Brontë's Inferno

Ewan Lawrie

Non

Non-U/KDP

Copyright © 2023 by Ewan Lawrie

All rights reserved.

No portion of this book may be reproduced in any form without written permission from the publisher or author, except as permitted by UK. copyright law.

Contents

Epigraph	VII
Foreword	VIII
1. Not a 419	1
2. The Mysterious Mr Mitie	6
3. Not The Two of Spades	11
4. "All Things Happen for a Porpoise"	15
5. Kobold	20
6. The Oldest Pub Still Open	26
7. Art For Art's Sake	31
8. Down Girt! Down!	36
9. A Few Pages Short Of A Novella	41
10. No, I Said	45

11.	All Of Them	49
12.	Special Instructions	52
13.	Sharon With A 'C'	56
14.	As Writers Often Do	60
15.	Gaga By That Time	65
16.	All The Terrible Books	70
17.	Probably In His Underpants	74
18.	I Was Thirsty	78
19.	Alligator Lizards On The Way To Malham	83
20.	The Sphinx Principle	86
21.	"Com-for-ta-ble"	90
22.	Enough Room For Hattie Jacques	94
23.	The Full Vincent	98
24.	"I Don't Dream of Dollars"	103
25.	Parma Violets	106
26.	Moonlighting	110
27.	Perhaps I Shouldn't Have	114

28.	All of Ken Dodd's	118
29.	"I Blame Cellini"	122
30.	"They're Not ALL mad"	127
31.	It's Just Lazy, Isn't It?	131
32.	Not-Rosa's Gnashers	135
33.	"If you know you are dreaming..."	139
34.	"You!"	143
35.	Did It Make a Difference, If You Couldn't Tell the Difference?	147
36.	That's What We Fools Do	151
37.	The Broad Arrow	155
38.	Just Like That	159
39.	"A-har, har, har."	164
40.	Not Even Purgatory	168
41.	"What kind of beast do you think I am?"	173
42.	The Lucky Ones	178
43.	"Or you wouldn't be reading this"	183

Epilogue

'At this point, I made the most injudicious error one might make in the company of a writer; that is, I encouraged him to expound further.'

Alasdair Moffat, Brontë's Inferno
Rafe Sabatini

Foreword

This is a book about a book.

It is also a book about books. All the books there ever were and all the books that ever will be, but particularly about one book that won't.

Alasdair Moffat is not the protagonist in this book, but the protagonist of the book that this book is about. No characters in this book, living or dead, exist on the temporal plane AKA in real life.

Readers over 40 years old may not need the footnotes: read them anyway.

Chapter One

Not a 419

I was in the town, behind a cold coffee and my battered lap-top. The older of the two staff in The Old Fire Station Café kept glancing over and failing to catch my eye. The coffee had been cold for a while. Probably since my mini-mouse had devoured the pathetic one hundred words that my first mug of most-definitely-not-smooth white whatever-chee-no had coaxed onto the screen. It was ten o'clock. Tea-breaking builders would be in shortly for hot drinks, and hangover-curing bacon in a tea-cake, but not a barm.[1] Not this side of the Pennines. I wasn't writing. I couldn't. Not since my publisher dropped me. You couldn't blame them, I'd sold enough books to fuel a fire, as long as it didn't have to keep anyone warm for longer than five minutes.

Untethered had been a brave, but ultimately foolhardy, experiment in publishing. At the same time, it was, for around two hundred would be reality TV stars – I mean writers – the last roll of the loaded dice in the last chance saloon. And as we know, the house, particularly Dodo Adventitious House, always wins. But, as we also know, though it may be rigged, nevertheless, it's the only game in town. Whatever, it was a blow when Untethered said "Thanks, but no thanks" to the third of my lovingly-created pastiches of different Victorian-age writers, "Brontë's Inferno." So I had a book I couldn't get published and no money to sink into its cov-

---

[1]. For the Metropolitans amongst you, this is a bread roll, usually a large one and definitely not whole grain.

er-design, editing, proofing, type-setting, or even bribing small independent bookshops into stocking a copy of it.

  Mug drained, I ordered another coffee in a plain white mug, knowing it would be a long wait to get one once the builders came in. Besides, I wanted the vicarious thrill, in the form of the smell of frying bacon, of the cause of someone else's future cardiac event. Sure enough, minutes later Roy came in, gave me a bluff nod and ordered enough rolls and pig meat to feed however many it would have taken to build HS2. Roy had ripped out the decking from the back yard at home, knocked up a couple of benches. He'd done the job as a 'tweener', something that would take a day or so, whilst the next big job came up. It was the first time I'd never given tea to builders on a job. They had sweated in the masks and taken them off after an hour, but they wouldn't touch my mugs. Sometimes, I wonder how we didn't all go mad. Then I read the newspaper and think perhaps we did. Roy's order was ready in no time, the Old Fire Station had been expecting him too.

The screensaver was on the laptop. Yes, a photograph of a copy each of my books, the time I'd put them on a shelf in Waterstones and snapped them with my phone, just before I was escorted out by someone who probably had a manuscript somewhere in the ether or under the short leg of a writing desk. In limbo somewhere, anyway. I pressed the return key. Why make the log in difficult? Who was going to steal three unfinished novels and "Brontë's Inferno"? Precisely.

There were some notifications: three tweets about bats in Berkshire, a retweet of one of my own about finishing BI, and quote-tweeting me luck with it, a dozen Facebook posts with pictures of cats, and e-mail from someone called "Valteri Mitie", subject 'An Offer. Not a 419[2]. Read this,

---

[2]. 419 is the Nigerian Criminal Code number for the advance fee letter scam.

what's to lose?' I must confess, I had always been interested in these scams. I sandboxed the e-mails from time-to-time, but still wouldn't click on or through. I used to enjoy the spelling. I was disappointed in Valteri's e-mail, there weren't any spelling mistakes. When I opened it, all it said was,

'I'm finishing a meeting. One signature and I'm done. Stay there.'

I stayed there. What would you have done?

Chapter Two

The Mysterious Mr Mitie

I WATCHED THE TWO people the management of the café believed sufficient deal with a steady parade of builders, social workers from the council's child care unit next door, nail technicians and barbers. Meanwhile I waited for the mysterious Mr Mitie. By the time I finished the second coffee, it was a quarter to eleven and the rush was over. I stood. I always paid my bill at the till. The brother and sister sharing griddle and customer relations duties looked young enough to be my grandchildren, if I had had any. I had just handed over the cash when the door opened and the cold January air made me shiver.

'Ah'll 'ave two of whatever Mr Sabatini's havin".

I turned to look at the person who had used my pen-name, rather than – well, it doesn't matter now. The mysterious Mr Mitie's apparel belied his accent. He wore a long, military-looking greatcoat, not threadbare by any stretch of the imagination. Except for the buttons, it could have been the one my father used to stride about in, at RAF Catterick[1], many years before. The greatcoat was open, perhaps to cut a greater dash, as it swashed, as in buckler, when he stamped his knee high boots on the coir mat in the doorway. I almost laughed at the jodhpurs. I half expected a monocle and a flying helmet. I'd have said the man was around 60, except for the barely lined face and the luxuriant –

---

1. Once the RAF Regiment's training depot. Now Catterick Garrison. My father's punishment posting for upsetting a bigwig officer.

if grey – hair. The man made a shoo-ing motion with his hands, clearly expecting me to retake my seat at the cheap and unmatched table in the corner. I did, but with a reluctance I was somehow unable to escalate into any kind of refusal.

The young man brought over the two not-whatever-cheenos just as the man was taking his seat opposite me. He slid his coffee to one side and leaned forward, elbows on the table, fists under his chin. I looked at him, feeling disinclined to start the conversation. He gave a slow nod, which moved the fists a little and I almost laughed.

'It iss easier if I sspeak a language they know.'

Any accent at all would get you strange looks in a town like ours. Mine always did, and there was no trace of the latinate in it. Still, his dalesman's schtick was exemplary, though it did no good. I could see the two Arkwright siblings in the small kitchen, pointing at Mr Mitie's outfit and whispering. They'd be telling customers about him for a month.

'Mr Mitie, I presume?' I said, any verve in my conversation had disappeared with my ability to write.

'I amm a kind off explorer, yess, you could ssay that.'

I couldn't place his accent, it was as though a Scandinavian was doing a Bela Lugosi[2] impression. But I wasn't going to ask him. Where he was from, I mean. That question had been on enough lips, since before Brexit. Besides, I didn't really care, I was thinking about which of the other four cafes in town I was going to be using from now on.

'How did you know my real name?'

I took a sip from the instant coffee and burnt my mouth, while I waited for him to answer.

'Nothing is ssecret nowadayss. Now ssacred, that iss another matter.' He winked,

---

2. Respected Hungarian stage actor who became a merchant seaman, before jumping ship in the USA. Universal's original and best Dracula, responsible for how Ygor is depicted in any Frankenstein moving picture, appeared as Dracula later in Abbot & Costello Meet Frankenstein (qv), his last credit was posthumous for Plan 9 From Outer Space.

actually winked - and I saw that his skin was only unlined because it was stretched so tightly over his face.

'Where would the profane be without the ssacred?'

Chapter Three

Not The Two of Spades

'What do you want, Mr Mitie?' I looked him in the eye. His seemed to reflect a flickering flame that was nowhere in evidence. The taut-skinned man laughed. It was the hoarse bark of a wolf who had serenaded the moon until sunrise. 'It should be pronounced "Meet-y". However, it iss not my name. No more than yours is "Sabatini"[1].'

---

1. Rafael Sabatini, Author of 'Scaramouche'. The kind of book that's no longer written. Perhaps you think that's a good thing. I couldn't possibly comment.

Valteri "Meety"[2]. I thought about that, later. I remained silent, remembering terrible police procedurals where not saying anything made the suspect run off at the mouth like silence was the ultimate truth drug. In the spirit of truth telling, I should mention that I couldn't think of anything to say. The man's chin was still supported by his fists. Though he held my gaze, I could not help but feel he was looking through me, although the passing pedestrians on the other side of the café window were surely not *that* interesting. I finished my coffee. He held up two fingers without turning to look at Amanda or Kyle Arkwright. I hadn't seen him drink any of his coffee, but the look on Kyle's face when he replaced the mug told me they hadn't either.

'Well then, I musst tell you it's not a matter of what I want. No, not at all. It iss mosst definitely a matter of ... what *you* want.'

'How did you find me? What are you, some kind of Data Miner?'

---

2. A heavily accented rendition of "Walter Mitty". No doubt his own little joke.

E-mail to real-world meeting in under an hour. I hadn't even replied to the e-mail. It was enough to make you believe in vaccine chips, almost.

That laugh again. If he did it when passing a dog in the street it would be fight or flight for Fido, for sure.

'I told you: nothing is ssecret.'

He made a pass with an open palm over his mug and produced a card. Not the two of spades[3]; a business card, which he handed to me. Red embossed print on thick black card, it read:

'Editor-@-Large,
Charnel House Publishing
chernobog@tchort.ru'[4]

He took out a jewelled toothpick and poked it fiercely around an overlarge canine, not bothering with the covering hand. I didn't see him put the toothpick away either.

---

3. In cartomancy, the two of spades means someone is going to be cheated. Probably you.

4. Don't write to this address. It's a Russian e-mail. That's RISKY!

'Your wish, your dream, your ambition, it iss to see your books published? Or to sell millions? Do you want fortune? Or fame?'

I told him a little of both would be nice.

'Ah, but you know that both are not possible. Not for you. You only have talent. This iss never enough. It hass not been enough... Well, you know for how long it hass not.'

Elbows back on the table top, he steepled his fingers, and I knew he was about to tell me a lie.

Chapter Four

"All Things Happen for a Porpoise"

'Your latest book iss magnificent.'

'So magnificent my publisher doesn't want it.'

'All things happen for a purpose.'

It came out like "porpoise", I stifled a snigger and wondered if anyone had ghosted

Flipper's autobiography[1] back in the day. The Editor's face changed, the eyes flashed, his cheeks becoming more prominent although I had not thought that possible. Maybe I'd smirked, surely he wasn't reading my mind?

'You can make a living from writing. We can help you. We have helped people like you ... many timess.'

'Oh, I get it. You're one of those vanity publishing scammers. Pretty bold turning up Eye-Are-Ell, fellah.'

He surged forward in the chair; my coffee spilled, the mug rolled off the table and shattered on the tiled floor. Maybe the café had been the Old Fire Station's lavatories. He sat back just as suddenly and began to laugh.

'IRL – in real life. That iss very funny. No. We are not a vanity publisher. Far from it. We do not want your money.'

He punctuated each word with an outstretched index finger. It pointed at my heart. Thanks be, said finger wasn't loaded.

---

1. Flipper was a US-made TV series about a delphine version of Lassie or Rin Tin Tin, or that bloody annoying kangaroo. It was rubbish.

'But you do want something?'

I finally found out what "askance" really meant.

'Well, don't you?'

If he didn't say something sensible I was going to be on my toes and back home creating new accounts for everything from Facebook to Fox News. Maybe I'd leave that one be.

'Everyone wants something. Whether it iss what they need iss another matter. I – We would need you to become invisible.'

'Oh yes? You know what that would cost in bandages?'

'You try my patience, Mr ____.'

He used my real name for the second time. No-one knew that the Rafe Sabatini who had written 'Kyphotic Hall' and 'Mississippi Moffat' was really me, not even the people who worked at Untethered. Most had moved on, and with those that hadn't I had used a series of cut-outs that Le Carré would have blushed to include in anything about The Circus. No, I was the second best kept secret in publishing, after the mysterious Italian woman who wrote books about not very much.[2] No-one knew me and no-one cared, except The Editor and I – and I wasn't too sure about me.

'Mr ____, I think you know very well what I mean. You would be expected to eraisse your on-line life. No profiles anywhere. Nothing. You will become a kind of ghost writer.'

'How much? I'd need a lot to write a footballer's autobiography. It's not the writing, see. It's the listening to the self-centred struggle to express themselves.'

'What about a bottlenose dolphin?' Again that humorless laugh. Perhaps he was a mind reader.

'£100 a click.'

'I wass joking. No, we will publish your work under entirely fictitious names –'

'Been there, done that.'

'Not like this.'

He stood suddenly. I flinched.

---

2. Oh, you know the one, Ferrante. Sold millions, and no-one has a clue who they are...

'Keep the card. You will call me. I can meet you anytime… ' He looked around. The Arkwrights busied themselves in the kitchen.

'But maybe not here.'

Chapter Five

Kobold

The Editor left the building and disappeared into lunchtime comers and goers. At the counter, I waved a fiver at the Arkwrights and they waived the bill.

'We're not licensed for other business...' Amanda said, and they both shrugged, as awkward as teenagers at a wedding disco.

I nodded, getting where they were coming from.

At home I napalmed Rafe Sabatini's on-line presence, just as soon as I'd downloaded all the data everyone from Zuckerberg to FailingWriters.com had on him. Or was that me? Sometimes even I didn't know. Then I changed my VPN provider to one from a company in Turks & Caicos. I kept my real name e-mail address. I hadn't used it in five years, except for (non-)royalties statements from Untethered[1]. That makes it sound like it all took ten minutes. It didn't.

A week later, I'd taken my life in my hands by descending the leaf-mulched stone of The Cat Steps. I was walking through the woods. The bare trees were nice, though better in the spring of course. I went to take in the brutalist architecture of Hullen Edge, with its oblong-block outcrops and regular shaped caves. When the sun peeped through the canopy, the yellow stone looked like desert pattern camouflage. Not so striking in the winter, but still magnificent, apart from the litter.

---

1. This publisher is a figment of my imagination and as such bears no relation to any publishers trading or bust. Or I'm a figment of theirs...

I saw movement in the largest cave, the entrance was twelve feet by three. It looked like someone had removed a large piece of stone for some or other henge. I went closer. A bent figure emerged. Although he was far too old, he was dressed like a journeyman "auf der Walz".[2]

There *was* something of the Harz about the Edge. The man straightened as best he could and held out a hand to shake, he went for the Masonic move and I dropped his hand.

'Ach, it is all nonsense anyway. I am Kobold[3], I work for The Editor.'

'Pleased to meet you,' I said.

'Are you, really, Mr _____?'

---

2. As recently as 30 years ago, German journeymen – you know, carpenters, stonemasons, those people who did all that stuff that no more than a handful of people actually does nowadays – used to wear a mediæval outfit with leather trousers jacket and feathered hat.They would become itinerant tradesman for a few years. **Auf der Walz** means "On the wander".

3. Kobold, old Germanic root English word for Goblin. Particularly one that worked in mines. Apparently his name is Daten Kobold. Daten is German for Data.

Perhaps I wasn't that pleased, especially since he knew my real name. Kobold gave a slow nod, then took a deep breath,

'I have been looking for you.'

'Found me then, haven't you?'

He gave a phlegmy cackle as if the breathing the fresh air had irritated his throat. 'Not yet, I haven't, but I will. No-one can hide from me. No dark web portal is closed to me. Your VPN won't protect you.'

'It will slow you and Charnel House down. Eventually, The Editor will look for someone else.'

He laughed again, then spat.

'He wants you. Besides why wouldn't you take the offer? It is the best deal. Beyond your wildest dreams.'

There was the tell-tale ping of something arriving on a mobile. Kobold took out something that looked like an ancient Nokia but clearly wasn't. He used a pointed fingernail as a stylus on the tiny screen.

'Ha! Once again I live up to my name. Good morning, MickeyBulgakov@mailbox.pro.tc '

Kobold turned the screen towards me. The display seemed to float in the air above the phone. There was an email composition window. From, To and Subject were filled in.

> From: Datenkobold@LeichenHaus.com[4]

> To: MickeyBulgakov@mailbox.pro.tc

> Subject: Meeting Today at Fleece Inn. Now

Kobold's long fingernail typed faster than I could with two thumbs.

'Better go, Mr _____, he's waiting.' Kobold scuttled into the cave and was lost to the darkness three feet in. I turned on my heel and headed back up The Cat's Steps. I'd be in The Fleece in ten minutes. Daten Kobold would find me in less time next time. I wondered how rich a company Charnel

---

4. German for 'Charnel House'.

House was, when it had tech that I'd never even heard of.

Chapter Six

The Oldest Pub Still Open

People say The Fleece is the oldest pub still open in the Calder Valley. People say it's haunted too. I'm not sure which I believe less. It *does* look old – outside and in. Outside it looks as though it was built in stone quarried from the Long Wall cliffs at Hullen Edge. Inside, it is a collection of small dark rooms, where the wood has the dark shine of the polish of years' worth of backsides. There are beams and low ceilings; walls are as straight as an arthritic finger; some of the seating would not look out of place in a mediæval church, whilst the rest are mismatched and mostly wheel-backed chairs. The floors are stone, save in the function room, which is barely larger than any of the other rooms, but does have floorboards. The most modern thing is the computerised juke on the wall next to the room that barely fits round the pool table. You can't play darts and pool at the same time.

At 12.15 on that Tuesday I hadn't expected the Fleece to be busy, but it was empty, save for the manager behind the bar and the now familiar silhouette of The Editor in the shadowy far corner of the snug. I gave the manager a nod and he placed a pint of Guinness on the bar.

'Tha' maits paid.' He glanced over at the figure in the corner.

I picked up my pint. There was no shamrock in the head, just a crudely drawn eye.[1] I

---

[1]. It was the Eye of Fatima. I had to look it up. You're not obliged to, of course.

looked back at the counter, but the manager had gone through to the main bar.

'Forgive me for not sstanding.' The Editor said, as I approached the table in the corner. He had a half-finished wine-spritzer in front of him. I almost wished I'd arrived earlier to hear him order it. He indicated the wheel-back chair on the opposite side of the table to his church pew.

'Sso, have you decided to accept my offer?'

'What offer? You haven't made one.'

'Are you sure about that? Have you checked your new e-mail?'

'Not since this morning.'

'Mickey Bulgakov! I remember him. He knew a thing or two about publishing. Isn't it funny?'

'What?' I wasn't laughing.

'Funny how the sshop is clossed in publishing whether it's capitalists or communists in charge.'

He took a sip of his spritzer. He had one long fingernail, just like Kobold's.

'Self-publishing. Have you thought of that? Samizdat[2], old Mickey called it.' The Editor barked his laugh again. A dog from the flats behind answered. The man went on.

'Imagine! If he'd lived to see the day, I mean. All that self-publishing we have now. Instead of dissidents overturning the status quo, we have millions of disenchanted would-be writers clogging up the internet. He would have laughed 'til he cried.'

'So what? I'm not going to self-publish. I can't afford it.'

'Charnel House can. We are a real publisher. Even the wizard woman is – ha ha – "on our books". A slightly different case, I grant you. All you have to do is give up the right to be acknowledged as the writer, of anything. You will get ALL of the money. ALL of it. Think of it, overseas rights, merchandising tie ins... MOVIE RIGHTS. '

---

2. Samizdat – or самиздат in cyrillic – actually means self-publishing. It was a dissident, not to say illegal, activity in Soviet Russia and the Eastern Bloc in general.

This last was so loud, some of his spittle landed on the bottle-scarred table, next to our drinks.

'No-one will know it's my work?' I asked.

'Has anyone heard of you now, Mr Published Author?'

Chapter Seven

Art For Art's Sake

We sat silent for a while. Then The Editor stood, his white-wine spritzer still half-full, as my pint of stout was. He gave me a brusque nod, for all the world like some character from a long-running soap leaving "t' pub". On the way out, he slapped the side of the computer-juke, by the time he was gone, John, Paul, George, Ringo and

Mr Martin[1] were listing all the reasons why they wanted to be a paperback writer.

My latest burner phone trilled, an SMS. It was a dumb phone. It couldn't read e-mails, Whatsapps, Tweets, Facebook or palms, much less fingerprints. Nobody had the number. I'd only bought the 'phone that morning in town, at the computer and mobile shop next door to the last independent optician's for fifty miles around. I knew Raj, the owner at Elland Electricals, well enough to nod at in the street and he knew me well enough not to ask many questions about why I needed yet another phone. I didn't recognise the number, why would I? I had put no-one in the address book, which was actually just a directory for phone numbers and names, if they were short enough. I thumbed the unfamiliar keypad. A terse message appeared on the tiny screen.

---

1. The Beatles, quite a successful beat combo in the 1960s. Ask your grandma. She'll either go misty-eyed or light up a spliff and say 'I preferred The Stones'. (Another beat combo).

> 'Meet Enoch 06.30 at the Cricket Ground. Bring contract. Kobold.'

The Guinness downed, I shouted through to the main bar that I wanted another, but not before thumbing buttons on the computer-juke until I found the song I was looking for. I sang along, bellowing out 'Gimme your body, gimme your mind' to the accompaniment of 10cc's[2] usual chord complications. By four o'clock I was drunk and had been "offered outside" twice by people who didn't care for my musical taste, much less my singing. I went home to sleep it off.

At one o'clock in the morning, I was wide awake, listening to night-time's soundtrack of the M62 traffic hum on the hill top, punctuated by the sound of sirens further down the valley. I went downstairs, keeping my head very still. In the porch, on the

---

2. '70s band noted for their literate, often funny, pop/rock. Ask Grandad, Dad as applicable.

mat, was an A4-sized packet. It must have been a tight-squeeze through the letter-box. The address was hand-written in the kind of copperplate that hadn't been taught in schools since the teachers stopped hitting the left-handed's knuckles with a ruler.[3] Why it had been addressed at all was a mystery, since it had clearly been delivered by hand whilst I was asleep. I made some coffee. Whilst the pot was on the gas, I inspected the packet closely. There was no return address on the reverse. It appeared to contain both paper(s) and something shaped like a book. The coffee made the racket that always reminded me of a well-known breakfast cereal's reaction to the pouring on of milk, recorded at low-level and blasted out on a speaker turned up to 11. It hadn't used to be so noisy, when I'd bought it. I poured myself a large mug and let it stand on the occasional table next to the sofa. It would be too hot for another fifteen minutes.

---

3. This was still happening in some schools in the 1960s - not in the Home Counties, of course. In Scotland, the North and in Ireland. I know, right, "they had schools?"

As I had guessed, the papers in the packet were the contract. Boilerplate written in copperplate. It was odd that Charnel House had Kobold and some beyond the cutting edge tech at their disposal, but chose to draft a fifteen page contract by hand, in ink, on some very expensive paper. A slip of paper was enclosed, the kind of thing printed up to put a short note in some official correspondence that doesn't merit any real communication.

'Be there.' It read, and next to these two bare words, there was something that might have been initials, or a stylised drawing of a goat's head.

The book - of course it was a book – was handsomely bound in cloth and leather, There was no dustcover, with a garish picture reducing the contents to the lowest common denominator. The book was called Brontë 's Inferno, and the name underneath it was Valteri Mitie.

Chapter Eight

Down Girt! Down!

WELL, OF COURSE, I spent the next six-or-so hours wondering who the hell Enoch was. A salesman to deliver the persuader? The convincer? The real deal clincher? Or someone else? The cricket ground was only a brisk ten minute walk away, five minutes past the Fleece, along Hullen Edge. So by the time my fake antique mantel-clock struck the quarter after six, I'd drunk enough coffee to raise a dead man. I was singing to myself, I often did,

BRONTË'S INFERNO

when abroad in the early hours. An anti-social habit perhaps, but I truly did not care. In fact, I even hoped that anyone woken up by my off-key – even more than Mick's[1] – version of 'Time is on My Side' would be humming it all day.

I limbo-ed under the barrier blocking the entrance to the cricket ground. It was long pole that wouldn't have looked out of place at Checkpoint Bravo, at Dreilinden, where I used to drive out of West Berlin, to cross the badlands of East Germany. Maybe Enoch worked for the KGB?[2] Maybe Charnel House thought Brontë's Inferno was a spy novel. I had an unpublished collection of stories on a hard disk in the bottom of a drawer about being a kind of spy in Berlin. Life-writing, one might call it. Or mental masturbation. I would read them every so often, just to

---

1. Jagger, lead singer of the beat combo The Rolling Stones. One of only two original members left. Very wrinkly, but not as wrinkly as the other one.

2. KGB, former employer of Russia's President-For-Life-Any-Minute-Now Putin. Nowadays known as FSB, think MI5/6/CIA run by gangsters.

see how bad they were. I'd put them on line about fifteen years before. Even MI5 weren't interested, although I'd broken the Official Secrets Act at least three times.

It was 6.25 by my knock-off fitbit. Time *was* on my side, I could see no-one. It was dark, the sun would not be up for another hour. I wondered where the "meeting" would take place. Perhaps, no-one would come. Who was called Enoch, nowadays, anyway? Unless, their dad was a BNP supporter.[3] I found a stray cricket ball at the foot of the scoreboard building. If no-one came, I would leave the unsigned contract – dead drop-fashion – on the bench by the nets and pitch covers – with its red leather paperweight on top. I set off on a circuit of the whole ground, for want of anything better to do.

---

3. Refers to Enoch Powell. Made a speech that was somewhat controversial about immigration about 60 years ago. Some say he was right. But I haven't seen any rivers of blood anywhere.

In the opposite corner of the ground from me, there was a pedestrian access gate in the high stone wall. Someone came through it, I registered there were two distinct shapes. One humanoid and the other what looked like the outline of a very large canine. Quite how large, I found out with in a few seconds. The hound dashed towards me and then it was front legs down barking up at me, loud enough to wake the dead, or at least the residents of the hospice over the road from the cricket ground. A rotund figure approached somewhat less rapidly, crying out something like 'Girt! Girt!' between gasps and coughs. I stood very still, not sure of the dog's "Bonio fides". The barking continued. I would have covered my ears with my hands, but I was still carrying the contract and the book. The dog had a brindle coat with markings so pronounced they gave him the look of a tiger. Finally the gasping owner arrived, and shouted as best he could,

'Down, Girt, down.'

The dog complied.

'Girt? What sort of name is that for a dog?' I asked.

The man puffed his chest up slightly, although it didn't diminish the corporation he carried before him by much,

'His name is *Girt Dog of Ennerdale*.'[4]

I somehow doubted the beast was Kennel Club registered.

---

4. A dog believed to have killed between 300 and 400 sheep in the fells of Cumberland, England, from May to September 1810.

Chapter Nine

A Few Pages Short Of A Novella

T HE DOG CALMED DOWN at the uttering of his full name, rather in the manner of a Gerry summoned by an irate mother shouting "Gerald". Indeed, he went to Enoch's side and stayed at heel as we walked over to the bench by the scoreboard building. By this time Enoch was panting again. I suggested we take a seat, though the wood was cold and damp.

'Have you signed it then?' He said.

'I haven't even read it.'

I tossed the contract in his lap. I had taken great pleasure in punching a couple of staples through the corner of the document, so fine was the paper. It was only missing a watermark to make it a still greater waste of money.

'I shouldn't worry, it just boils down to you not being famous, but being very rich... and the other thing, of course.'

'What other thing?'

'Oh, you know, the usual. Do you like Stravinsky?'

I didn't care for Igor much and said so. Enoch looked disproportionately put out,

'Oh ... I thought you might at least have liked The Soldier's Tale[1] , you being an ex-military man.'

'I wasn't a soldier.'

'That's the kind of detail that we don't consider so important. Some of the guidelines haven't been changed in centuries. Hoplite,

---

1. Dark Faustian fable about a deserting soldier and the Devil who eventually possesses his soul. Isn't the internet amazing?

Soldier, Airman, same difference. Besides, you'd be an aviator now, wouldn't you?'

The Air Force had cancelled the word "Airman", deciding to call all other ranks "aviators", regardless of gender. That was fine, you couldn't stop progress. Trouble was if you said aviator to me I'd picture someone in jodhpurs, goggles and a leather helmet. Yes, Amy Johnson. I wondered if anyone had mentioned the word 'aviatrix' at the MOD. They'd probably have thought it was something to do with S & M.

I grunted a reply. The dog growled.

Enoch scratched his chin and sighed.

'They sent me to convince you. Well I'll tell you this : I didn't sign and ended up working for Charnel House anyway.'

'How's that?'

'Not out,' he laughed. 'I've been there a long time. I'm famous. My book's in the Apocrypha[2], if you know what that is. I've met nearly everyone in the world and half

---

2. Books that could have been in the Bible but aren't. Why am I telling you this? That's what the internet's for!

the people in publishing, although as you've probably guessed, they're not all... people.'

I knew my coffee had been strong, but I'd never heard of caffeine-induced hallucinations before. Perhaps Enoch was simply mad or madly simple. Everyone I'd met from Charnel House seemed a few pages short of a novella.

Chapter Ten

No, I Said

Enoch gave me an old-fashioned look and Girt gave a low, rumbling growl.

'Don't tell me you'd rather be famous?'

'Why not?'

'You spend a lot of time hiding behind *noms-de-toile*, for someone who wants to be famous. I mean, Mickey Bulgakov? Puh-lease!"

I wondered what a *nom-de-toile* was. It must have shown on my face.

'I always think *toilette* would be a better word for the web, don't you?' Enoch raised one eyebrow, à la Roger Moore.[1]

'I'd rather be both.'

'That's not the deal,' he said. 'Have you heard of Justin James?'

'No. It sounds like a boy band member.'

Enoch guffawed, 'Might well have been at one time, sometimes they called him James the Just.'

I heard the faint tinkle of a very small bell.

'His brother was much more famous. Still is, although he's dead, we think. Justin James is unbelievably rich though. He gets royalties from half of the best selling book in the world.[2] People think Saul Damask wrote most of it, after he changed his name. He was a thug though, even afterwards. Not keen on women as I recall.'

---

1. Actor who played The Saint. Was the Funny Bond, after the "Shcottish" One and before the Boring One, not counting George who was just in one film and played him like The Milk Tray Man.

2. The second half.

BRONTË'S INFERNO

Enoch took out a big fat doobie and lit it, as though he was some big-shot Hollywood producer lighting a cigar, instead of a fat man on a wooden bench at a village cricket ground.

'I really do wish I had taken the offer. I'm tired of wandering. And being a one-book wonder. Me and Harper Lee[3]. Famous, right? Not rich though. Comfortable, at best.'

'You must be more than comfortable, if you can afford to feed that dog.' I looked down at Girt, who was salivating.

'He gets his own food. He's famous for it.'

'Famous, eh. None of his paw-prints on a contract then?'

Enoch took another puff and offered me the joint. I shook my head. It was about time I told him I'd never heard of him. So I did. He was incredulous, to say the very least. 'But, but you're the guy who wrote Kyphotic Hall[4]

---

3. Wrote 'To Kill A Mockingbird' and kept a half-finished book in her bottom drawer, which of course her publisher inflicted on the world after her death.

4. Not the book's real name, but he was right, there was an Enoch, just not him.

You put me in it. You must have heard of me?'

'I'm sure I didn't, although there *was* an Enoch.'

'Well, there we are then.' He blew some mary-jane smoke in my face.

'You're a little tall. This Enoch was a person of restricted growth.'

'Based on me then?' His bottom lip protruded.

'He was a scientist. Although more the type found in monster movies. Are you of a scientific bent, Enoch?'

'I don't think much of science. It's all people trying to prove stuff that other scientists say is wrong. I prefer religion and superstition, you know where you are with those. What you believe is right and everyone else is wrong. Am I right?'

'No,' I said.

Chapter Eleven

All Of Them

Enoch stood, brushed at the damp seat of his trousers and gave a short whistle. The dog ran over to the opposite side of the cricket ground and sat down at the gate the two of them had come in by.

'You can keep the book. I assume you have looked inside already?' he said.

I had. And I had got it. That feeling. You know the one, the one where you see your words, your actual words, in a real book. I had opened random pages and gloried in the feeling. Even though it wasn't my name on the cover.

'Don't look inside it again, until you get home.'

It was a strange thing to ask, but I nodded, grunting an 'OK'.

The man straightened, suddenly seeming less corpulent, lither than before.

"The Editor will be in touch. And that will be the third time of asking, won't it?'

I was trying to think of an answer but he had already walked straight across the hallowed ground of the cricket square itself and I thought what the groundsman would have said if he'd seen him.

It was full daylight. The traffic hum had started and the birdsong had stopped. Or been drowned out by the cars and lorries and buses taking people and things from there to here and back again. A car marked Elland Taxis almost ran me over as I stepped onto the zebra outside The Fleece. I saluted a single magpie as I turned onto my street, he winked at me and I winked back. Back in the house, I made more coffee and took it upstairs to the office, along with my book. The cover no longer had Valteri Mitie under the title. My name was there. I opened the book at page 402. It was blank. As was page 13, 42 and 66 at the start of chapter Six. All of them, all of my precious words were gone.

A slip of paper fell out from somewhere between the pages. "Compliments of Charnel House" it read, with the stylised initials beside it, looking more like a goat's head than ever. I took my coffee downstairs and poured it down the kitchen sink. My burner phone rang, the display showed a "Baphomet"[1] was calling from a concealed number. I let it ring out. Then I poured a stiff gin, though it was only nine in the morning.

---

1. I don't know how to pronounce this either.

Chapter Twelve

Special Instructions

I FELL ASLEEP AROUND half-ten. An hour later I woke up. Someone was hammering on the front door or my head. Or maybe both. I stumbled to the front door, tripping over the walking boots I'd left in the middle of the floor. On the other side of the front door was Andrej, the DPD guy. For a change he wasn't trying to leave me with a delivery for someone a dozen doors down.

'For you today. Is important I think. Special instructions.'

He held up the piece of paper he held in his hand. The package was on the ground at his feet, its stiff cardboard soaking up water from the puddle on the concrete. I hadn't ordered anything, unless I'd been drunker than I thought, in the last week or so.

'What special instructions? Something to sign is it?'

'No. Is read this papers.' He waved the paper and I saw that it was a single page.

'But no signing. Nothing to sign.'

'Yes, but just usual, that both sign. Is funny, isn't it? Never have special instructions like that before. I wait, you read.'

The single page had two dozen-or-so lines of the usual Charnel House documents' copperplate on one side only. So I read them, but not out loud, you understand.

"Here is a box. It may be empty, it may not. You cannot know until you open it. But then you cannot know whether it was empty when it was shut. It may have contained dreams,demons or disco biscuits. Any or all of these. If you open the box, they will es-

cape. If you do not they will find a way out and leak slowly into your life. Or not. One thing is certain, there is no cat inside this box. Imagine if this box contained everything outside it. Imagine if it contained only string, or sub-atomic particles, or quark, strangeness and charm. Imagine yourself as Pandora. Or Pygmalion. There is no limit to what might be in the box.

Until you open it, of course.

Consider this a gift, conditional on signing the contract when we meet again later today. You will be unable to open the box, until the contract is signed.

Until later'

It was signed with the – by now familiar – goat's-head-shaped initials.

'That's it, I've read it. Now what.'

'I take selfie with you, Sir.'

'Proof of delivery. Or that I've read this?' I shook the paper at him

'No, you might be famous. Ordinary people don't get special instructions.'

We posed for the camera.

'I don't think I'll ever be famous, Andrej.'

'Not even 15 minutes?'

Then he gave me a delivery note, from a carbon-papered pad, of which we both signed the top copy. The box was still intact, though its bottom was soggier than on a Celebrity Bake Off loser's victoria sponge. I looked at Andrej's signature on the paper in my hand: child-like letters, full and round, carefully arranged on the paper.

Andrej Warhola[1] waved as he got back in the white van.

---

1. If you need a footnote to get the joke, you're reading the wrong book.

Chapter Thirteen

Sharon With A 'C'

I KNELT ON THE lounge floor beside the soggy box, still out of breath from carrying it in. I heaved it the other way up. It hadn't looked so heavy. No wonder Andrej Warhola had left it on the ground. And now, soggy-side up, the cardboard was drying before my eyes. There was no heating on in the house. It was too expensive, that was why I was still wearing the coat I'd worn to the meeting with Enoch. It was cashmere, and still had the scratchcard in the secret pocket that the people in the charity shop hadn't found. Maybe I'd check it one day, but while it was still in your pocket it could still make you rich. Once you'd scratched the paper film away, it was just so much cardboard.

The *box*'s cardboard was stout, sturdily old fashioned. It wasn't marked fragile. As a matter of fact it wasn't marked at all. No address, nothing. The tape on the box was old. It looked as though it had dried out in the way that cellulose tape does, but I tugged at a ragged edge and nothing happened except a flake of dried tape fell onto the carpet. The box remained firmly shut. I fetched my Swiss-Army knife from the office upstairs. Then I ran the longest blade along the centre of the tape holding the top – or bottom – of the box closed. It was like running the blade through sand, no sooner had the tape parted than it closed behind the blade. I brought the point of the blade down as hard as I could on the cardboard, jerked it out and the cardboard regenerated like a sea-cucumber's gonad.[1]

Just then the mobile beeped like a 50's sci-fi robot. I fished it out of a pocket, there was a message, terse but succinct. It read,

> 'Told you not to open it until after.'

I pushed the box to a corner of the room and put the waste-basket on top. Then I collapsed into the sofa, picking up my battered copy of "Earth Stopped"[2] on the way. There wasn't anything Arthurian about it and the prose was 1930's dull, which was why I had been reading it for a month. Besides, it was about world devastation after a disaster, and who needed that? Before I knew it I was asleep and dreaming I was an ant.

The doorbell went just as Merlin was changing me into a badger. I dragged myself

---

1. They do. They really do!

2. A deservedly minor work by T.H.White. All four vol.s of The Once and Future King are much better. So good that Disney made a cartoon out of volume one. Which wasn't so good.

to the door, stuporous as an airman on a night shift.

It would be a lie, if I claimed to be expecting a peak-capped chauffeuse standing outside the front door, much less the Rolls she had parked, blocking the whole of Consort Street. I was at a loss as to how she had manoeuvred the limousine down the narrow thoroughfare, between all the cars that never seemed to go anywhere. She said her name was Sharon with a 'C', and that Charnel House had sent her.

I told her I didn't have an obol[3] on me.

---

3. An Ancient Greek coin... Keep up!

Chapter Fourteen

As Writers Often Do

Charon drove the great yacht of car down the side-street and doubled back behind my back yard and in front of the low-rise flats as though she was in a Mini Cooper in Turin. I heard the champagne flutes rattling in the Phantom V's cocktail cabinet all the way to the Cold Edge Road. I popped the catch and took out a glass and a piccolo of the Widow,[1] figuring there'd be less glass to rattle that way. Charon caught my eye and winked at me in the rear-view mirror. The glass divider had been open since before I'd got in the car, although Charon had remained silent until now.

'Only way to travel, Sir. Would you like some music?'

'Why not? You choose.'

She held up an eight-track cartridge with Chinese characters on a faded label showing a group of figures that could have been The Beatles or The Banana Splits.[2]

'I like this,' she said.

It wasn't either of them. Deep Purple Mk II[3] encouraged Charon to drive even faster as she turned up 'Highway Star' so loud my fillings rattled. I almost spilled my fizz, when she hit the zed-bends on the rise out of Ox-

---

1. Veuve Cliquot - a bit recherché, beggars, choosers and all that.

2. Not a beat combo, just four guys dressed in what appeared to be NFL mascots' outfits.

3. The best incarnation of this popular beat combo.

enhope. I was relieved when we reached Haworth. She finally slowed down, letting the Phantom V purr down Changegate before we turned off onto Church Street and pulled up in front of the BPM: The Brontë's Parsonage Museum.

'Here? You do know it's not open on Tuesdays?'

'Of course.'

Charon got out of the car. Perhaps the uniform was a good idea. *Anyone* who drove like she did was liable to hauled over by traffic, much less someone of her heritage. I wondered what was under the Phantom's bonnet, it had seemed to travel faster than anything that size had any right to. The driver opened the rear door, for all the world as if I was a visiting dignitary, albeit one wearing a second-hand cashmere coat and baseball boots.

I walked up the path to the entrance. The Editor-at-Large stood on the threshold, arms wide in welcome, as though he'd been waiting forever to see me. We went inside. I'd been before. I remembered being suspicious of the whole thing, wondering how much was set-dressing and what furniture actually stood where it had two hundred years ago. The Editor ushered me along the entrance hall, we turned right through the kitchen and went into the library, with its sign reading "by appointment only". There were two club-chairs facing each other over an occasional table. I had no idea if they were there permanently, never having made an appointment. The Editor indicated that I should sit, and took the other chair himself.

'I thought we'd conclude our business here.'

'Why?'

'We tried to contract them, you know?'

'Who?'

He sighed, the taut skin seeming almost transparent.

'We weren't called Charnel House then. We have had many names. From the first incunabula to E-books, our name has changed with the times. Our names are legion. As are our writers.'

His dog bark laugh turned into a coughing fit.

'We thought we might get Emily, but no – none of them signed in the end.'

'Only Emily wrote just one book. Anne and Charlotte, they wrote several.'

'Precisely, and who is the loser?'

Not for the first time, I pondered The Editor's sanity. As writers often do.

Chapter Fifteen

Gaga By That Time

The Editor-at-Large was wearing his military greatcoat, jodhpurs and boots again. However, this time he had outdone himself by adding a white shirt, bootlace tie and and a rather foppish silk waistcoat whose design I couldn't quite make out, thanks to his voluminous coat. He reached for an inside pocket and brought out another sheaf of paper with the beautiful script written out on one side of the sheets only.

'This iss the third time of asking, Mr _____. You will find it an improved offer.'

'I'm not very good with all that party-of-the-first-part stuff. Why don't you tell me what's changed?'

He shrugged and gave a slow nod,

'Not much. There ain't no sanity clause[1], for example.'

This time dog-bark laugh was positively explosive, shattering the quiet of the Brontës' library. I sniggered, despite myself.

'No, seriously, though. It iss a better deal... well, than we have given anyone.'

'It's still the same choice though, Fame or Fortune?'

He steepled his hands, something which looked strange as the occasional table was too low and fragile for him to lean his elbows on. He looked like he was going to pray or bow his head and say 'namaste', instead of telling me a lie.

---

1. The Contract Scene in A Night at the Opera – no not that one – The Marx Bros. film. You Tube it, I know it's in black-and-white. So what?

'Well, it is ... and it isn't...'

'How's that?'

'You will get both, but – let us say – you will have both for a limited period only. Your innings will be relatively short.'

This was followed by an unsteepling of hands and a rather effete clap.

'How short?'

'It could be as much as twenty years.'

'How does it pan out? You can't be famous and suddenly not famous.'

'Oh but you can, Mr _____. Your deal will be similar to the schoolboy-wizard woman's, but better, oh yes, but much better.'

'She's got that pseudonym everyone knows about though.'

'Not for long, Sir, not for long.'

'She's still famous – well, infamous now.'

'I refer you to my previous answer.'

The Editor stood up, went over to some piece of furniture that looked the right age but the wrong design and fixed us both a drink. Brandy, in something the size of a spaceman's helmet. He sat down.

'You know, the internet is the finest thing humankind has ever invented. You can be king of the world one minute and -'

He paused to make the inverted commas with his fingers,

'the devil incarnate the next, before disappearing as though you were never alive. Cancelling. It has been so good to us at Charnel House.'

'How will my deal be better?'

'You will be twice as rich and twice as famous as - what's-her-name.'

Perhaps he *had* forgotten her name.

'What's the catch? There's always a catch.'

'No catch, you will simply continue writing after the fall. It won't be exactly the same. You'll be providing celebrities' murder mystery novels, sports-people's autobiographies, politicians' memoirs, that kind of thing.'

I knew that would make me 80 years old give or take, by the time my twenty years of glory was up. I reckoned I could be gaga by that time. So, just for something to say, I asked,

'How many of these books would I have to write?

I saw The Editor-at-Large smile for the first time. His teeth were sharp pointed, small and now all the same size, as though he'd had implants made in the shape of a gin trap.

'All of them.' He said.

Chapter Sixteen

All The Terrible Books

The Editor-At-Large had acquired a battered looking fedora from somewhere. He performed a graceful doffing just before I saw him disappear into the Gents. I waited twenty minutes before assuming it was a dismissal. I thought about checking the cubicles, but didn't. He might have left a window open as he left, but I had the distinct feeling he hadn't – and I didn't want to know for sure. On the table in front of me was yet another sheet of paper with the now familiar script. There wasn't much on it. A pair of sentences, the whole consisting of several lines, each with a hand drawn box beside them, in which one further sentence exhorted me to place a cross, a tick or any suitable mark in one of them to indicate my preference, and to sign at the foot of the page.

"I hereby agree to the conditions of the contract in full: to wit that, after twenty years, I shall work in whichever location Charnel House or its next iteration chooses, writing all the terrible books deemed necessary by The Editor-At-Large regardless of whose name appears on the cover" ☐
"I agree to replace Enoch, both as Wanderer and guardian of Girt Dog Of Ennerdale" ☐

I crumpled the paper into a ball, threw it towards a receptacle marked litter. Naturally, I missed. An insubstantial old fellow appeared, wearing a cow-gown, such as a farmer or veterinarian might use. He'd as well have been accompanied by a flash and a puff of smoke, so suddenly did he materialise. He bent down to pick the ball of paper up and handed it back to me. I stuffed it in the breast pocket holding his three coloured biros and called him a rather impolite name. A man's patience has its limits.

As fate would have it, Charon was on the point of entering The Parsonage Museum as I was preparing to exit. I was almost knocked off my feet, but she was swift enough to catch me as I fell.

'No funny business, Mister.'

It truly was some time since I had contemplated any sort of business of that kind, funny or otherwise. I was quite flattered that she considered me capable of any behaviour that might be considered less than appropriate. Then I reflected that I would never be her partner of preference in the matter of funny business, in any case.

I allowed Charon space to effect her exit before following her to the Phantom V. The car had remained untouched. Perhaps Haworth had fewer disenchanted youths than Harehills. Or any that they did have, had been frightened off by my driver. Goodness knows she frightened me, and not just with her driving.

One mustn't form the impression that Charon was in any way unattractive. Indeed, in younger days, I would have spent many a happy hour contemplating her jodhpurs and boots, how she filled them and how to get her out of them. Those days were long gone, of course, and, furthermore, who would have dared offer any compliment at all, for fear of repercussions?

Charon slammed the door with somewhat more force than necessary, as I was making myself comfortable in the back of the Rolls. Was everyone a mind-reader nowadays?[1] I noted that the glass between chauffeuse and passenger was closed. The tiny cocktail cabinet had been replenished, heaven knows how, so I cracked another bottle of fizz, just to pass the time.

---

1. People of your esteemed author's age often say things out loud when they only mean to think them. Thanks to a sizeable minority of senior citizens, we are **all** labelled "racists".

Chapter Seventeen

Probably In His Underpants

Just past the junction of Victoria Road and Jepson Lane, the road was blocked by two patrol cars, so there was no way to reach Consort Street by Mini, never mind in a Rolls the size of the one I was travelling in. There had been little conversation on the way back from Haworth. I was a little woozy from the Widow. The last piccolo was in my coat pocket: the three empties were on the plush carpeting in the foot-well. Charon opened the window between driver and passenger. Her breath smelled of cinnamon. Her head jerked backward, so I presumed that mine didn't.

'I'll have to drop you here.'

'It was nice to meet you.' I slurred a little.

'If you need me –'

'Just whistle. Yes, I know how to whistle, thanks.'

'Use the number on your 'phone. "Underworld Limo Hire".'

She got out to open the door for me, oblivious to the honking of Elland Taxis, Ubers and Ocado delivery vans lining up behind us. I didn't bother asking how that number had ended up on my dumb-phone. I had no doubt Kobold had worked some dark magic in a room with no-windows and arrays of servers against the walls – probably in his underpants.

I watched the Phantom V tear down the rest of Victoria Road and take the corner onto the Huddersfield Road with a fishtail turn that I took as a sardonic farewell gesture. On Consort Street, about half-way down, there was a smouldering pile of rubble where number 35 had been. It had been a two-engine fire. It must have been the fastest response in the history of Elland, if not of the "West Yorkshire Fire and Rescue Authority". I walked down the street towards the barrier tape marked "WYFARA Do Not Cross" and hopped nimbly over it, if I say so myself.

The nearest firefighter loomed over me, I could see several bristles on her chin.

'Get back behind the barrier, Sir.'

'That's – was – my house.'

'Did you leave the gas on?' Her tone was sufficiently accusatory as to make me think I had, and to show that she thought so too.

I stuttered a reply in the negative, anyway. Looking bemused at the space like the void left by an extracted tooth between the two houses.

'How come my neighbours' houses are undamaged? That's hardly possible, is it?'

'When did you last check your boiler?' Another firefighter said.

This one's hi-vis tabard read "Fire Chief". I suppose that's what you get when an "authority" deals with fires, instead of a brigade. I shrugged.

'It's your own bloody fault then, isn't it?' Bristles said. This was accompanied by some spittle some of which landed on her boss, who stepped backward and stumbled over something on the pavement behind her.

When she recovered her balance, she pointed at what she'd tripped on and said,

'It's not the only thing that's hardly possible at this scene. We found that where the living room used to be.'

She was pointing at the mysterious box delivered by Andrej Warhola, only 24 hours before.[1]

---

1. Look no footnotes... Oh, darn it!

Chapter Eighteen

I Was Thirsty

'Do you have somewhere to go, Sir?' The chief asked me, demonstrating an unexpected solicitude given the circumstances.

"Course 'e han't. People in these 'ouses ain't got two pennies t'rub together.' Bristles gave her twopenn'orth[1]. proving she felt herself a cut above me and my neighbours.

---

1. If reading this outside Yorkshire, it means tuppence-worth. That's 2p. Probably a good valuation of most people's opinions, one might say.

But I had. I didn't keep – hadn't kept – vast amounts of cash in the house. Who did? I kept two hundred in twenties in my wallet as walking around money, but I rarely spent any of it. As for my neighbours, they couldn't afford walking around money for the most part. If they suddenly had two hundred pounds in cash available, they would spend it on luxuries, like fresh fruit and maybe a decent cut of meat or two. If they were downsizers, like me, they wouldn't keep money in the house. Too tempting for burglars, though there hadn't been a break-in on Consort Street since I had moved in. I gestured at the Fire Chief with my lap-top messenger bag.

'I've got this. That's all I'll need.'

The Chief nodded. 'You live alone? No-one we might find...' Her eyes darted towards the sodden pile of ashes that had been my home.

'Nobody? No, no body there.'

I gave her credit for laughing at my feeble joke.

'Well, Sir, there may be a Police investigation depending on what else we find.'

'What about the box?' I nodded at the cardboard, untouched by the flames and strangely dry already.

She didn't answer for a moment, perhaps the mind-reading was catching, I knew she was thinking the strange box would complicate a straightforward – if catastrophic – house fire, and that if I took it away there would be much less time and paper wasted on the incident.

'Take it,' she said. Bristles spat on the ground, quite near to the box. Maybe she'd breathed in a bit of smoke and ash. I hoped so. The box felt lighter, but looked exactly the same.

In the Fleece, there were a few customers talking about the fire. I overheard snatches of conversation about the day's events as I took my Guinness (no eye this time, just a wonky shamrock) to a table.

I took the one beside the digital juke. I missed the old ones, with the 45's you couldn't play on a Dansette without an adaptor, a bit of round plastic, or those bits of plastic that looked like shiruken that ninjas threw about in old films and early video games. I thought it was a pity The Fleece didn't let out rooms. There must have been room enough upstairs, even with the landlady living over the shop. Still, what if it really was haunted?[2]

My laptop was on the table. I bet myself it would be ready to go by the time I needed another pint. It took two, but I was thirsty. I started looking for a place to stay. I wanted something in the dales, not in the Calder Valley's towns. I picked something that looked affordable. It was out of season, I doubted it would be busy. I booked it through their web-site. In the name of Mickey Bulgakov. Why not? It was as good a name as any and I had it as an e-mail address. Then I phoned Underworld Limo Hire on my burner. Got an answer machine: told them where I was and where I wanted to go. I hoped they'd

---

2. I have no idea if the Fleece is really haunted, but – interestingly – there is a post funeral wake/bun fight every other week. Perhaps the guests of honour hang around for a while afterward.

send Charon, just because I wanted to see people's faces as she hunted the warren of rooms in the pub to find me.

Chapter Nineteen

Alligator Lizards On The Way To Malham

I HEARD CHARON before she got as far as the room with the digi-juke. Well, I heard the smashing of glass and a high-pitched gurgling sound. I went through to the bar. Thankfully, all the smashed glass was on the flagstone floor, and not rammed at the tattoo-ed guy's neck. Maybe the dark stain around the crutch of his paint-flecked jeans indicated the glass had been full, rather than his bladder. There were beads of sweat on his shaven head, running down the inked iron-cross on the back of his neck.[1] Charon's leather-gloved hand was holding the thug by the throat, keeping him shoved against one of the sepia photographs that hung so high on the wall it was getting its first dusting in decades. The landlady was polishing a glass that was already clean, looking like she wished she could have a cigarette instead.

'You, Mister,' Charon was saying, 'are ten thousand generations nearer to being a monkey than I will ever be.'

With that she gave the Neo a final shake of the throat and let him drop in a heap on the glass-littered floor. She turned to me and smiled,

'Now then, Sir, where would you like to go.'

Because I have always been careful, I said I'd tell her in the car.

The window between Charon and me was open.

---

[1]. I realise this guy is a bit of a cliché, I've met many nice people with tattoos, and I bet Suella Braverman hasn't got one.

'Quo Vadis, Imperator?' she said.

'Isn't Charon a Greek name?'

'Greek, Roman, what does it matter, when the empire has fallen?'

'I'm going to stay up at Malham Cove for a few days.'

'Hotel?'

'One of those holiday rental things. Shepherd's hut.'

Charon put the Rolls in gear and steered the Phantom V smoothly out of The Fleece's eight-space car park. The window between us stayed open. I put my hand on the back of the shotgun seat in front.

'Sorry about that, in there. Lucky he was on his own, eh?'

'He sure was.'

She pushed a cartridge into the 8-track. Not Deep Purple this time. America... Ventura Highway. I thought to myself I'd keep an eye out for alligator lizards on the way to Malham.

Chapter Twenty

The Sphinx Principle

WE WERE CRAWLING UPHILL on a one-and-a-half lane road. The rain was biblical, the two sheep and a dog looked like they'd missed the memo from Noah, we had to stop so they could get past. I wondered what the Rolls's immaculate paintwork looked like now. Charon's face was like the thunder which was the only thing missing from the storm outside. The Phantom V felt all of its two-and-three quarter tons. I was glad I wasn't driving. We had passed the

Beck Hall Hotel five minutes ago, but it was still visible out of the rear window. Perhaps I should have booked a room there.

I tapped Charon's shoulder,

'How far now? And don't say round the next corner, I'm not five.'

Charon gave a sound half-way between a laugh and a grunt.

'Sat Nav's gone haywire. It said about a mile away as we passed Beck Hall...'

'About half-a-mile, then?'

I saw the shrug of her shoulders when she said, 'Maybe.'

'Anyway,' I felt like talking. To take my mind off the weather – and whether it would stop us reaching our destination. 'How come the sat-nav is kaput? I thought Kobold was Charnel House's tech genius.'

The driver stole a brief glance over her shoulder.

'I don't work for Charnel House. Nor does Kobold. We're sub-contractors. Underworld Limo Hire is me, I am a limited company. Most demon-' She cleared her throat, 'people are on zero hours contracts. Charnel

House and The Editor-At-Large were way ahead of the game on that one.'

'Still, I'm surprised the SatNav doesn't work.'

There was a flash of lightning outside, I was half-way through saying 'one thousand' in my head when the missing thunder arrived.

The metalled road ran out. There was only enough gravel for a single track "road".

Charon braked and switched off the engine. The *Son et Lumière*[1] show was still going on outside. The even heavier rain meant there was nothing visible beyond the Rolls's windows.

'I'm not driving into mud when this gravel runs out. You'll have to walk. Last I saw of the SatNav's map it's at the end of this track. Bethesda Pool Farm, wasn't it? '

'I'm not going out in this.'

---

1. There's a reason why the outdoor show has a French name, Sound and Light sounds dull and any outdoor performance doesn't go well with the capricious nature of British weather. Unless it's Glastonbury.

She gave me a look like she was Jules Winfield. I hoped she didn't have a gun – or a bible.

'There's a sou'wester in the boot. I'll pop it for you, but I'm not getting out of the car.'

Jules would have said 'trunk', I thought.

I watched the car reverse slowly down the gravel until the rain made the Rolls disappear like God had used the Sphinx Principle in his latest magic show.[2]

---

2. A very famous illusion back in the very olden days, before Dynamo. By Thomas Tobin, who wasn't even a magician but a scientist.

Chapter Twenty-One

"Com-for-ta-ble"

I TRUDGED UP THE track, glad that I'd left the mysterious box in the trunk. Charon could deal with it. I'd no doubt she'd contact the Editor-At-Large with the news that I'd palmed it off on her, as slick as a music-hall cardician forcing the two of spades on a small town spinster. I leaned into the driving rain, half-expecting to see some demented Emily Brontë fan channelling Kate Bush[1] and running hell for leather down the hillside, without actually wearing any shoes. The rain was falling faster and heavier still, but at least the lightning had stopped. However, the landscape was deserted: up ahead I thought I could see a five-barred gate, but it could have been anything at all.

The sou'wester was a little too large, my baseball boots would never be truly wearable again. I *had* seen a gate: the padlock and chain looked like something for locking a beast in a cellar. There was a stile at the side and I entered the field, slipping and sliding as I tried to keep hold of my messenger bag. Part of the grass was worn where a tractor had been driven over it, but not any time within the last year. I followed the trail uphill. At the end of it stood a farmhouse and a couple of buildings that could have been anything from stables to milking parlours,

---

1. Very famous British shantooz, sometimes thought to be a bit bonkers but just expressive. Had a big hit - long before Running Up That Hill in Stranger Things - with Wuthering Heights.

for all I knew. A huge and decrepit generator stood outside, juddering for all the world as though being soaked in the rain had given it the mother of all chills.

I made my way to the door of the farmhouse and attempted to use the knocker in the shape of an gnome's head. It had rusted to its plate, so I hammered hard on the door. I was about to take shelter in one of the outbuildings when the door opened with a creak that should have been in black-and-white.

I gave a gasp when the door opened to reveal a woman in what used to be called the prime of life. Well dressed, too, in the kind of trouser suit women wore on American TV in police procedurals. Her hair was long and very dark except for an arresting white stripe.

'Mr Bulgakov? For the Shepherd's Hut?'

She held out a hand:

'I'm Hella, very pleased to meet you. I'm sorry, but the hut has not done well in the storm. I would be delighted if you would stay in one of the farmhouse's bedrooms. In the far wing. It is quite private. Really.' There was something exotic about the way she turned the 'w' of 'would' to 'v'.

An eye-tooth strayed over her lower lip, whilst her eyelids closed and then opened again, slowly.

'Do stay, please. I'll do my very best to make you...' She took a deep breath and then exhaled all the way through saying "com-for-ta-ble".

Chapter Twenty-Two

Enough Room For Hattie Jacques

I COULD TELL YOU I was looking at the decor, the sconces with those faux-candle electric bulbs and the stained wood wainscoting; the holes in the thin balsa gave the impression of a long-abandoned set for a Hammer film.[1] I could, because I did – for as long as it took to notice. I thought about the Editor-At-Large, wondered what his and Charnel House's stance on The Male Gaze was. Then I did some male gaze-ing. The balsa-wooded corridor was about as long as a cricket pitch. We had just about reached the stumps, when Hella looked over her shoulder at me and winked. Maybe she wasn't too bothered about what I'd been looking at.

'It is just through here,' she pushed at a door that swung like a branch end leaf in the wind. It must have been balsa-wood too.

Hella waved me in with an arm that should have been draped in a Lily Munster[2] sleeve.

'I hope you vill be...'

'Com-for-ta-ble, yeah I get it. Maybe I will, as long as that bed isn't a film-set prop.'

---

1. British Film Production company, Schlocky horror movies marginally more scary than 1930s Universal ones, with more bosomy female characters. Hey, it *was* the 1950s.

2. The Munsters : a down-market Addams Family rip-off. It was funny though. Addams Family? Wednesday on Netflix is a distant relation, the programme, not the character, obvs.

'I voz going to say, joining us for dinner.'

'Us?'

'Oh, just the old gang.'

'Ma Baker's? Ned Kelly's? The Sugar Hill?'[3]

'You are making the jokes. Splendid, laughter is the best medicine... especially in the dark.'

I half expected the generator outside to give up the ghost and the house to be plunged into darkness.

Hella brushed past me on her way out, although there was enough room for Hattie Jacques to get by and leave fresh air between us.

The bed was the real thing, at least it didn't collapse when I tossed my bag on the counterpane. A four poster, with tapestry drapes and a tester that were at once both faded in colour and begrimed by time. The finials atop the columns almost reached a ceiling that seemed improbable, judging by the apparent height of the building, when viewed from outside. Perhaps it had seemed

---

3. In order; US depression era gangster & Boney M song title, Australian Owl Hoot, rapping's original gangstas.

smaller due to the rain and the dark. There was more wainscoting. It looked identical to the mock-up stuff in the corridor. I gave a tap to a panel next to a washstand that was even older than the bed looked. It was the real thing, or an imitation so accurate it didn't matter. I gave the panelling a shave-and-a-haircut knock just for luck, as if I were "an American, already".

I looked at my watch. It showed a quarter past five. Dinner "vould be at 8", with some dreadful spirit as an aperitif, a half-an-hour earlier, no doubt. I threw myself on the bed and landed on my messenger bag. I was asleep in minutes, despite the pain in my kidneys.

Chapter Twenty-Three

The Full Vincent

I must have been sleeping like a whole cabin of logs, for when I went over to the ancient wash-stand, the porcelain had been replaced with much newer pieces. And the water in the jug was still hot, too. I'd heard no-one enter, perhaps I'd heard them leave, but the balsa-wood door to the room was hardly going to make much noise, unless it actually broke.

Taking the water's temperature as a hint, I made an attempt at a submariner's shower and rearranged my clothing thereafter, thinking the creases in my shirt gave it quite the unstructured look. Scruffy, some people call it.

I didn't remember taking my baseball boots off. Or cleaning them. When it came to thinking about it, they looked new.

The cricket pitch corridor had about five doors to each side, leading off it. Most were locked and these were of traditional construction, meaning that they were not made of balsa wood. The 9th door was not locked, but was made of enough balsa to make an architectural model of Whitby Abbey, before it was a ruin.

I went through the ninth portal. [1]

The room was off, I saw that straight away. A door should have been to my left about nine feet from the one through which I had entered. There was no other door into the room but the one on an adjacent wall that was an improbable distance away. Again

---

1. Clue. I should have expected Judas, Brutus and Cassius on the other side.

the ceiling seemed to be making a lie of the building's roof. A long table was set for twelve diners, but there was no-one seated. An enormous fireplace was on the wall opposite, which was also at an unlikely distance. Before the fire were three high-backed club chairs of the type in which Vincent Price or Elvira[2] might be sitting to introduce some old black-and-white monster movie.

The chair backs faced me. I could see one was occupied. The person seated was singing a song I knew but in a language I didn't. He finished his performance and stood. As I should have guessed, it was The Editor-At-Large. He did have a velvet-smoking jacket on, but it didn't make him look much like Vincent – or Elvira, for that matter.

'Do you like London? I love London,' he said, with a cigarette holder clamped between his teeth. 'It's so full of rotters, cads and scoundrels. Especially, in publishing. It's just hea – perfect, for someone like me.'

He gave a yakking laugh and if he'd been trying to channel Terry Thomas[3], I'd have given it a nine out of ten.

'Now, I'm not offended that you have misplaced the package, oh no, don't worry. It's quite safe.'

He took another draw on the holdered cigarette and blew the smoke out of the side of his mouth.

'I'm not doing a deal with you or Charnel House,' I said.

'Oh Mickey! I can call you Mickey, can't I? Or Mihkail? You'd like that wouldn't you? Even your pseudonym's namesake did a deal in the end, you know.'

'Russian!' I pointed a finger at him. 'You were singing in Russian!'

'Da,' he said, 'What else?'

'Samisdat!' I shouted the only Russian word I knew. 'No deals for Mikey. The Stalinists didn't like him! Everyone knows that.'

'Do they? Do they really?'

---

3. British actor son of a Smithfield Market butcher. Specialised in upper-class cads, bounders and scoundrels.

'I'm going to self-publish too, actually.' I sneered.

This time it wasn't a yakking laugh. This time it *was* the full Vincent, I half-expected Michael Jackson to start singing.[4]

---

4. And the song would have been 'Thriller', mwah-haha-ha...

Chapter Twenty-Four

"I Don't Dream of Dollars"

THE EDITOR-AT-LARGE FINALLY RECOVERED himself sufficiently to speak.

'Self-publishing? It is a phenomenon, is it not. Belovéd of our Mikhail and of the spoiled fools of the West today. The foolish reactionaries of the Moscow intelligentsia peddled their piffling pamphlets and no-one read them and you and your ilk publish and damn yourselves to disappointment. What does talent matter? It is the least of it. The very least.'

By this time he was close enough to land a little spittle on my chin. It burned as though all the bile really were acid. He grabbed my left hand in both of his and leaned closer still,

'Take the deal. I am being more than fair. Riches, riches beyond your wildest dreams.'

'I don't dream of dollars.' I said.

'Doubloons? Ducats?[1] Dogecoin? DASH? Kobold could help you with those last two. I have an infinite supply of the others.'

He reached up behind my ear and produced a gold-coloured coin, flourishing it an inch from my nose before placing it in my shirt pocket.

I heard a scratching sound. It came from one of the other club chairs. A small black cat sprang from it and arched its back.

'Ah... have you met Beggy? I hesitate to say my cat, for Begemot is no-one's pet. The Russians don't like the soft aspirates much. They invariably change an H to a hard G.

I shrugged.

---

1. Old coins, found in books about Pirates and Musketeers respectively.

'Harry becomes Garry, d'you see?' The cat's shadow darkened the wall. It was huge, so yes, I did see. I bet myself Harry Sparkle would love that if he ever visited Moscow.

'What IS your real name? It isn't Valteri Mitie.'

'No, no, just my little joke,' he laughed. 'My name is Legion,'

I lifted a fist, but he stepped nimbly back, avoiding the cat by inches, though it hissed anyway.

'Okay, okay. Just call me Woland. How about that Micky B?'

'Why not,' I sighed.

Chapter Twenty-Five

Parma Violets

There was a scent in the air. Almost pleasant, but not quite. As though someone had lit one too many joss sticks to cover the smell of a particularly sulphurous fart. I felt quite sick. Woland, Mitie or whoever he was, was smiling; the sly smirk of a schoolboy who'd done the undetected dirty at the back of the class. He puffed out his cheeks and let out a concentrated blast of the smell. I wondered how he could believe Parma Violets[1] could fight the stink of his breath.

'So? What *is* it you want? Everyone has their price. Except me, of course. And the other fellow. He's not much bothered about anything now. Sometimes I wish he were. It was more fun, you know, when there were more of us. The classics. I remember that business with the swan, I wish I'd thought of that – '

'Nothing, nothing at all.' I said

'You must want *something.* I could give you a while to think? Come on, don't be embarrassed. I could tell you some of the things people have asked f – '

'I don't want anything I'm OK.' Even those few words were hard to say without breathing in.

---

1. Sugary sweets (US: candy) taste like the horrible cake thing in a urinal might.

'You're OK?[2] Good book that, I spend every day trying to provoke people who swallowed that guff. Not many of them left. Too busy not listening and just shouting. Where's the finesse in that, I ask you?'

It struck me that Woland was lonely, with only the cat and Hella for company, out here in the arse-end of somewhere everyone had forgotten about long ago.

'I want world peace, an end to famine and to fix the planet.' I sneered.

'I didn't realise you could be so funny. Would your books make me laugh?'

'I thought you had read everything.'

I had thought that. There seemed to no book – however obscure – but that he did not have some knowledge of it.

'I used to. But then you know... Those sportsmen's biographies, minor royals' children's books,' he looked as though he himself might be sick for a moment, before lowering

---

2. 'I'm OK, You're OK' – self-help book recommending the use of empathy before anyone used the word outside of 60's science fiction. The Post Office used it to train main office counter staff.

his voice to a whisper, 'the tv-show hosts' crime novels.'

'I thought that was what I was going to be writing for Charnel House,' I said, maybe a little too loud, since Woland flinched and then gave a shudder.

'Of course you will. But I will NOT be reading them,' he took a breath, 'Nor will anyone dull enough to buy them, I'm sure.'

'So that IS the deal. You publish Brontë's Inferno and I spend the rest of my days spinning dross into publishing gold?'

He laughed, actually laughed. If anything it made the stench of his breath worse.

'Oh no, Mickey B, you aim far too high, I will be satisfied if you spin dross into coherence, however uninteresting.'

Chapter Twenty-Six

Moonlighting

ONE OF THE CONFUSING doors opened and Hella walked in carrying a large tray that required the use of her full wing-span. Now she *was* dressed in one of Lily Munster or Mrs. Addams's cast offs. It fit her where it touched and it touched everywhere. Only the long split in the dress saved her from the geisha walk. It took me a while to notice what was on the tray, but once I confirmed I wasn't going to end up wearing the contents of it, I saw that there was a vast tureen that surely contained enough of something to feed at least twelve. There were four bowls beside it and some improbably neatly aligned cutlery. A long refectory table was at the other end of the room to the club chairs: it looked as though it stretched half the length of the cricket-pitch corridor on the other side of the wainscot-ted wall.

The Editor-At-Large and I both stood as if to relieve her of her burden, but Hella gave a tut and continued to the table. She placed the tray and its contents between two candelabra, badly matched for colour and height. As were the candles. The refectory table boasted only three further chairs in addition to the ancient throne at the head. These other chairs had matching cartwheel designs, although the one at the foot was also a carver. The editor swept a bow that directed me towards the seat at the foot of the table and then skipped – yes, skipped – to the seat of majesty at the other end. By the time I had sat down, Hella had served a bowl of something or other to Woland and the cat was sitting in the chair to his left, half-way down the table. I was served next. The bowl contained something that looked like *callos*, a Spanish stew of tripe and chickpeas that I had tried once in the Guadalhorce Valley. I wondered how much I would get away with leaving in the bowl. Hella served the cat, then herself and sat down opposite him.

Begemot was lapping at the liquor from the *callos*, a front paw either side of the bowl. Woland and Hella were picking out the pieces of tripe with thumb and forefinger, then slurping each one into the mouth like a child eating spaghetti for the first time. Or a chimp eating a caterpillar, for that matter. I thanked all the gods that never were that we each had a pair of decanters and glasses as part of our place setting. I sank near a half-litre of a singularly rough red from a glass that could have held a whole one. When I finished off the glass, I realised how they dealt with the chick-peas would haunt me for the rest of my days, and drank a half-litre of throat-searing hock from the other decanter. All three pushed their bowl away at the same time, liquor, chickpeas and tripe spilled onto the polished mahogany of the table, as though they had not eaten a morsel from them.

Woland stood and clapped his hands. The door opened. Charon walked in wearing a butler's uniform, with a starched collar and a stern look.

'Moonlighting?'[1] I asked her.

'I loved that programme.' Woland said.

---

1. What Bruce Willis did before Die Hard. The Thin Man (some movies loosely adapted from Chandler – not him!) updated to the 1980s, one critic wrote, regarding 'Moonlighting'. I know, you've never heard of any of them.

Chapter Twenty-Seven

Perhaps I Shouldn't Have

Charon ignored me and merely raised an eyebrow at Woland, who uttered one word.

'Vodka!'

Charon sketched a bow and reversed out of the door, gliding across the parquet floor without a sound. There was nothing resembling a drinks cabinet in the long room, in any case.

'Shall we sit?' Woland gestured at the club chairs.

If I was expecting Woland and me to be joined in the club chairs by the unnerving if beautiful Hella, I was sorely disappointed. Begemot, looking unaccountably larger than prior to his dinner of tripe, was sprawled across one, a pair of legs draped over each armrest. Hella stood behind Woland's chair, hands resting on the back, smouldering. Metaphorically, thank goodness.

Charon returned with a tray bearing a bottle of clear liquid and about fifteen shot glasses. She proffered the tray. Woland took the bottle and one glass. The tray was offered to me and I took a glass, too. Charon buttled backwards a step or two and then adopted a Jeeves-ian aloofness.[1] Until Hella cleared her throat. I thought I saw some smoke come out of her ears, but it must have been a trick of the light. Charon took a glass from the tray and tossed it towards Hella, who caught it and then laughed. Woland

---

1. Jeeves: P.G.Wodehouse's somewhat insufferable butler character, without whom Bertie Wooster would have suffered a fatal injury attempting to put his boots on the correct feet.

poured his own shot first. Hella leaned over the chair back and held her glass for filling. I looked away. Charon caught my eye and rolled hers. Then I held out my glass, which Woland filled well enough to form a maniscus, when the vodka reached the rim. I was surprised he didn't pour one for the cat.

My host shouted 'ваше здоровье'[2] loud enough to be heard in Elland and downed his vodka, before looking expectantly at me.

I necked it. 23 years in the RAF had taught me how to do that. But not how to keep it down without my eyes streaming. Woland hurled his glass into the fire. The remaining spirit in it caused the flames to burn brighter for a moment. He nodded at me. I lobbed mine weakly and it bounced off a log, leaving shards of glass on the hearth. Hella of course tossed off her vodka with barely an eye-blink and threw her glass backhand over

---

2. Russian toast, it means "your health". Perhaps in the hope you might still have some after several rounds.

her shoulder to the heart of the fire.[3] Charon had already presented the tray to Woland. I was somewhat apprehensive about another 100 proof shot. Charon leant towards me with the tray. She picked up a glass and dropped a pill in my lap, then winked at me. I made a better fist of dispatching my empty glass to the flames this time, using the distraction to swallow the blue pill Charon had given me.

Perhaps I shouldn't have.

---

3. I did witness someone attempt this once. It struck one of the pub regulars on the head and we were all barred *sine die*.

Chapter Twenty-Eight

All of Ken Dodd's

IT WASN'T THAT KIND of blue tablet. Although I suspected at the time Hella – for one – might have enjoyed it, if it had been. Nor was it knock-off valium. I don't know what it was. As for what it did... Well, it was like everyone else, maybe including the cat, had been pumped full of sodium pentathol. Also, I might have become invisible.

'That was a neat trick,' Woland was speaking, he sounded like Kenneth Williams. 'How did he do that? It took me millennia to learn that one.'

'Will he do it, Daaaaaaah-ling?' Hella really was smouldering, and she'd gone all Fenella Fielding.[1]

'I don't know. But we need a new writer. I thought he was so certain to sign. Writers – always so damnably awkward. Not like composers and musicians. Stravinsky and Paganini: so eager. I must say their enthusiasm for the novelty 45 r.p.m was tremendous. The Singing Postman's – all of Ken Dodd's: a fabulous effort by Eugène Scribe with Niccolo on that one about the violin by the way.' Woland said.

Hella nodded, murmuring, 'yes, daaaah-ling' into his ear.

Charon was no longer buttled-up. She was clad in a draped dress, possibly one last seen on Ursula Andress[2] in Clash of the Titans. She winked at me, pointed two fingers at her

---

1. Posh-voiced British actress of the 50s and 60s, finest hour as Valeria in Carry On Screaming. Enough said.

2. Also "The Girl From Dr No" referred to in 10cc's 'I'm Mandy Fly Me'.

eyes and waved one finger of the other hand at the rest in the universal sign language for 'but not them'.

I got 'What the f-' out before she shook her finger at me. So I gathered both of us might be invisible, but we weren't inaudible. Some crazy pill.

As for the cat, he now filled the chair, his back legs were crossed and he was smoking a pipe. In his other hand was a Tokarev pistol. The cat was speaking. I would have been lying if I'd said I was surprised that something called Begemot was speaking in Bernard Bresslaw's voice. It crossed my mind that the drug was a powerful hallucinogenic.

'I don't sink he's the right one. I should 'ave shot him.' The cat, with remarkable dexterity of paw, fired two shots into the ceiling.

'Oh do behaaaaayve, Beggers, love.' Woland said.

Hella, still behind Woland's chair, stroked The Editor's hair. 'Don't worry dah-ling. He'll come back. They all do.'

I glanced at Charon, jerked my thumb over my shoulder at the nearest door and mouthed 'Vamonos'.

She shook her head from side-to-side slowly, what she mouthed meant either that we couldn't or her opinion of me was disappointingly low.

Chapter Twenty-Nine

"I Blame Cellini"

It was like using a VR headset on ghost mode. Where you lurk about not touching anything, just watching all the other avatars in the game. It became quite the thing, among the dogging community during lockdown, so I'm told. Talk about ghosts in the machine. I bet Bob Sugarmountain hadn't foreseen that. I wondered why Charon had insisted we stay. Woland and Helle had moved on to bickering over the future of the verse novel.

'I dislike them intensely, Daaah-ling,' Hella's teeth seemed more prominent. 'Remember that Chaucer fellow? I found it wilfully obscure. And the spelling! When he read it to you, it sounded fine, but on the page? It was as though he couldn't decide on runes or letters.'

Woland gave a snort, some of the vodka came out of his nose, and then some blood. Hella's canines seemed to grow and I saw a flush creep up her cleavage. Charon cleared her throat very quietly, then Woland spoke, still spluttering a little.

'And that's why I paid a visit to Gutenberg. What a dump Mainz was then!'

Begemot hissed, 'Still isss.'

Woland gave him a withering look, Begemot didn't look withered at all.

'People don't like versse, becausse it iss hard.' The giant cat pulled his tail towards his mouth with a paw and then commenced to lick his rear appendage.

'Oh do stop that, it's disgusting.' Hella said. She must have found it so, as she forgot to add "Daaah-ling".

I rolled my eyes at Charon, thinking it was a good job I *wasn't* wearing one of those VR headsets. Why *did* no-one ever mention that they made everyone look like Cyclops from the X-Men? Charon pointed at Woland, then tapped her temple in the sign language for the well-used Yorkshire phrase "Think on't".[1]

Begemot left off his grooming, 'You need him, Woland. If he won't do it who will? All the real authorss have given up. You sshould neffer have signed up the first Sportsman. Aristotle[2] did a good enough job writing about the Olympics.'

'I blame the television, Daah-ling.' Hella said as she stroked Woland's cheek with her palm. 'Nobody cared about *anyone*'s private lives before then.'

'What about Augustine? Some people still read his now. Only students of Christianity,

---

1. Not to be confused with "wit kont" which may – or may not – be something frightfully rude in Afrikaans.

2. Ancient Greek philosopher who liked a drink according to Monty Python, [once the future of British Comedy, now barely on "speakers" and very grumpy old men.]

but still.' [3] Woland rubbed a finger along the side of his nose.

'I blame Cellini, though. Dull stuff, who cares about Benvenuto falling out with a Pope? What are Popes for, except to fall out with? Shame someone bumped Caravaggio off, now that would have been a block-buster.'

'Yess, but Cellini was the finesst ssculptor of the Renaissance', Begemot licked the back of his paw, 'You, Woland, saw fit to let Barnum[4] have his head. At least they were his own lies I suppose.'

Woland took a slug from the bottle, having run out of glasses. Begemot went on,

'We at Charnel Housse have fed the bonfire with mediocraties' vanity. Who wants to read a memoir "by" a diss-graced TV pre-

---

3. I'll let you look him up.

4. Either The Greatest Showman or the biggest carnival huckster ever. Maybe both.

senter? Not even Nabakov[5] could make that palatable.'

'But people buy them! We are adding to the sum of knowledge.' Woland was looking as red-faced as a bishop on a bicycle.

Begemot gave a stretch, 'Yet we are making it a zero sum.'

---

5. Wrote Lolita. No-one's real idea of palatable.

Chapter Thirty

"They're Not All Mad"

I was beginning to feel a little tired, as I had not taken more than a spoonful of *callos*, during the meal. I motioned again to the doorway behind me. Charon shook her head again, then held up a hand with fingers and thumb outstretched. I hoped she meant just five minutes more. So far, we had heard nothing that I did not already know, or had not deduced, by performing our disappearing trick. I wondered what revelation was supposed to ensue in the next five minutes. I wondered too, how this trick had been achieved. Was I hallucinating, or were The Unholy Trinity the ones doing the trip? Why was Charon also invisible?

Consequently, I had missed a further exchange between the cat and Woland. Charon's brow was ever-so-slightly wrinkled, perhaps in consternation. I resolved to pay more attention.

'There musst alwayss be a ssacrifice, you know that, Woland.' The cat had shrunk a little, no longer filling quite so much of the chair.

'Well, isn't that the problem? Why would anyone in their right mind make the one we ask of them?' Woland rested an elbow on the chair arm and cradled his chin with his hand.

'Isn't that why we choose writers, artists and musicians, Daah-ling?'

'They're not ALL mad, Hella.' Woland let out a breath that flapped his lips. 'At least not before they sign.'

The still shrinking cat's voice was heading towards a light tenor from his original basso profundo, 'Your Mickey B must be thinking he iss around the twist already, by now.'

'I don't know, there's something funny about this one. He's so phlegmatic. Nothing seems to surprise him. Not me, not you two, not Enoch and not even Uncle Tom Kobold and all.'

Hella had produced a cigarette holder the length of a car aerial. The cigarette was already lit. 'It will be fine. Remember the trouble we had with the Wizard Woman?'

Woland sniggered. 'Oh yes. And what a good deal that was. Never have I seen such ... Well, you know, the stuff we need to keep going. Our best piece of business in millennia.'

Begemot's voice had reached Hella's contralto range. 'The more there is, the more we need. The terrible books are a great metaphor, truly.'

Hella blew out a smoke ring you could have kicked a football through.

'- and don't forget, boooooys, he thinks that all the terrible books is the worst of it. He will crack and when we have him, well

– then all will be well, the status quo will pertain.'

And with that, the three of them, Charon, even the room, all disappeared. And I believed I might have too, whilst hearing a repetitive riff and some inane lyrics about down, down, deeper and down.[1]

---

1. The sound of Status Quo pertaining...

Chapter Thirty-One

It's Just Lazy, Isn't It?

I woke up in a hospital bed. I know, if you were reading a novel, you'd toss the book as far from you as you could. I know I would. I mean who puts that kind of thing in a novel? It's just lazy, isn't it? As though the author just couldn't find a credible way out of the previous scene.

Charon was by the bed, fiddling with something that beeped and buzzed and was connected up to various parts of me, she'd have got the part if she'd been auditioning for the part of Nurse Ratched in a remake of 'Cuckoo's Nest'. I cleared my throat, began coughing and then the beeps stopped, followed by a particularly annoying siren sound going off. Was this it? I wondered if the crash team were called that because they were so noisy, what with the trolley banging off the door and the edge of my bed. What happened next was shocking. No, I mean shocking. Anyway, the beeps started up again.

So, no clear white lights. Never mind, I wasn't a big fan of Lindisfarne[1], anyway. The crash team crashed out of the room although I couldn't hear any alarums coming from elsewhere. Maybe it was a hard habit to get out of, or they'd watched too much medical drama on the tele.

'What was all that about, Mr Bulgakov?' Charon's brow was furrowed, an effect I had thought it would have taken something built

---

1. Popular Geordie beat combo in the 70s, responsible for soccer nutter Paul Gascoigne releasing a single called 'Fog on the Tyne'.

by Massey Ferguson to achieve. until that moment.

'All what?'

You were brought in with a touch of hypothermia. Nothing too serious. That's your third seizure today. You were found wandering by a sheep farmer from Ripon way.'

'But that's miles from...' I stopped, not wanting to sound any more mad than this rather distant version of Charon already thought me.

'Yes, you were, Mr Bulgakov, miles from anywhere,' she looked down at the old-fashioned patients notes on her clipboard, 'And naked.'

'What the hell was in that pill you gave me?'

Massey Ferguson did their job again, 'What pill?' You've been on a drip since last night, Mr Bulgakov.'

I looked down at one of the cannulae, the one in the back of my right hand. There was something odd about it. I mean the hand. The skin wasn't crepe-y enough. Why was she calling me Bulgakov, anyway? I hadn't been carrying any ID with that name on. It was just the name the Editor-At-Large insisted on using. I'd never use it on a bank account. I doubt even an oligarch would. It was a nom-de-plume, a pseudonym, an alias, a disguise.

Charon pressed a button on the thing next to my bed and I watched the liquid all the way down the plastic tubing, through the cannula and then into the back of my hand that I didn't know anything like. Then I didn't know anything at all.

Chapter Thirty-Two

Not-Rosa's Gnashers

There was no sign of Charon in or out of the Nurse Ratched outfit, when I woke up. Rosa Klebb's[1] younger sister was dressed in a severe suit with a skirt and flat shoes. Luckily, I was in the hospital bed and not inclined to get out of it, so I didn't get to

---

1. Villain played by Lotte Lenya, a serious actress who worked with Brecht, and married Weill, but is mostly remembered for playing a scary Soviet [What we called Russians when they were the baddies... Oh, wait.] in From Russia With Love.

see if her brogues had the stiletto blade in the front. She opened her mouth and I could see she didn't have Soviet-Era dentition. No, Not-Rosa's gnashers had been bought at some high-end place in Hungary, the kind where you didn't come back with cranial neuropathy. Her gleaming white teeth did not make her any less scary.

'I call you, Bulgakov. Is good Russian name. You not Russian.' She produced yet another copy of "The Contract" from a large handbag, along with a Mont Blanc fountain pen. She laid the contract on my lap and unscrewed the pen top and jammed it on the barrel end. The woman proffered the pen nib first. Could she be an assassin? I asked myself.

'No is poison gas pen. Only special ink. Sign contract, I go.'

Maybe not an assassin, but a mind reader. I'm not that terrible a card-player: I once won Volkswagen Beetle at three-card brag and I hadn't even cheated.[2] The woman was still looking at me, unblinking, like a snake.

---

2. Honestly. The other guy thought I was bluffing but I was just drunk.

'I kill you, if no sssign. You not kill me. You not *Рикки-Тикки-Тави*.' Her laugh was guttural. 'Kha-kha-kha' like a she'd put the ending of "loch" on the front of the sound. I half-expected her to expectorate afterwards. Maybe the hissing on the sibilants was enough.

I signed, carefully, 'Mikhail Afanasyevich Bulgakov' in Russian script, then handed the contract back.

'You not khim either. You have contract official copy in box.'

'What box?' I said, though I did know which box she meant. The woman used her polished brogue to slide the familiar cardboard container out from under the hospital bed.

'Only bok-ssss that matter. Or anti-matter, Kha-kha-kha.' An excessively long tongue, split in the manner of some over-dedicated goth's, emerged from between her lips, , . 'Goodbye, Rikki Tikki.'[3]

There was something sinuous in her walk as she left the room. After the door closed behind her there was a scream and the clatter of something frangible hitting the floor.

   I got out of bed. I was going to look in the box. I'd signed now, after all. How bad could it be?

Chapter Thirty-Three

"If you know you are dreaming..."

T HE BOX WAS ON the bed, opened. There was no magic tape resealing itself this time, though it was definitely the same box. I hadn't unpacked it. A mirror still lay on the top of muslin-wrapping, but I hadn't got as far as finding out what the material wrapped. I had my back against the wall, as far from the bed as I could get in the small room. If I had been on a general ward, I'd have been a lot further away from the box. It was only the fact I was dressed only in one of those dreadful paper gowns left over from the rubbish Baroness Mone[1] had sold the NHS a couple of years ago, that prevented me being outside the hospital with my thumb outstretched. That mirror: I did and didn't want to look at it again. You can guess why.

Come on!

I did look at it again, sure. I picked it up this time. It was a hand mirror. The handle and frame, though tarnished, were far too heavy to be silver plate. It looked old. I supposed it quite valuable. You've probably guessed why I did look. Yes, looking back at me was a younger version of yours truly – though I had never been half so handsome. Like Dorian Gray's portrait[2] in reverse, my image showed none of of my sins, transgressions or peccadillos. I looked at my hand holding the mirror. A young man's hand. I remembered

---

1. Lingerie seller, alleged medical equipment swindler and – at the time of writing – life peer in the House of Lords.

2. Novel by Oscar Wilde, also known as Prisoner C.3.3. whilst in Reading Gaol for being homosexual. Yes, people did use to go to gaol – and later jail – for that.

noticing it when Charon had been playing Nursey. That had been before I'd signed the contract, hadn't it?

I returned to the open box. Pulled at the muslin, which hadn't been wrapping anything after all, merely covering the rest of the box's contents. Which were clothes. And not mine. The jacket I shook out of its precisely folded state wouldn't have fit me at the age the mirror was trying to convince me I was. I pulled the cord and baled out of the shoddy gown. If anything, my shape was more shocking than the face in the mirror. Suddenly – and for no justifiable reason – I was ripped. I checked the jacket for a label. It had an embroidered one, "**Alter és Kiss, Budapest**", but that meant nothing – bar its place of origin being Hungary – to me. There were trousers and expensive underwear and a white cotton shirt like one I had bought in the Bahrain souk most of a lifetime ago.

They all fit the new me.

"If you know you are dreaming, you're not really dreaming, that's the acid test." As somebody absolutely *must* have said once.[3]

---

[3] I can find no record of anyone ever saying or writing this, so it must have been me.

Chapter Thirty-Four

"You!"

It was no surprise to me that neither Charon-in-her-scrubs, nor Not-Rosa Kleb turned up when I pressed the big red button on the wheeled drip, drug assembly thing by the side of the bed. Nobody came at all, in fact. Since I was no longer connected up to that machine which was supposed to monitor vital signs, there was no audio alarm. The big red button was a bit of a con:

like the button over your head on a RyanAir flight[1], it was purely for decorative purposes only – and never likely to summon any kind of help at all.

The box still wasn't empty. The messenger bag containing my lap-top was in it. Now that *was* magic. Not because I hadn't seen it in some time. Rather because, until today, I had been unable to open the box at all. Somebody had, obviously. I chose not to dwell on the fact that the box had looked identical to the way I had last seen it, nor on the implication that there was much, much more than met the eye, when it came to the box. I put the mirror in a padded pocket in my bag, a little unsure why I did so. The last thing in the box, was the handsome volume entitled 'Brontë's Inferno', now with the name 'Mikhail Bulgakov' on the cover. I checked inside. 135,000 words, all mine, since Un-

---

1. In the olden days, flying anywhere used to be fun. No, honest. People would put on their best clothes to fly, and in-flight catering didn't come in Pringles tubes and Coke tins. Getting through security was not like visiting time at Broadmoor. Hard to believe I know.

tethered had turned it down sight-unseen and no virtual blue pen had desecrated my manuscript. Of course, that didn't mean I thought my novel was perfect, who ever does? I imagined the Editor-At-Large pointing his long-nailed finger at me and saying 'You!'.

Tucked in a pocket inside the back cover was a folded copy of the contract, as promised. My signature was at the bottom, although I knew Not-Rosa had taken the contract I had signed away with her. I turned to put the tome back in the box, intending to take it to wherever I was going to spend the next few days. I would find time investigate its construction a little further, later.

The box was almost full again. An old-school Royal AIr Force greatcoat was folded carefully. It smelled of moth-balls. The buttons were brass, but they didn't have the Shitehawk[2] on them, just the strange glyph that might have been a signature or the head of Baphomet, which appeared on all the documents connected with Charnel House. I dropped 'Bronte's Inferno' in the box and picked it up. I folded the flaps down and they stayed put. Then I walked out of the room and followed the signs to the Hospital exit. A sign on the way out told me I had been in the Calderdale Royal Hospital.

---

2. Actually an image representing an eagle, found on Royal Air Force shoulder patches and uniform brass buttons, Most service personnel used to call it a Shitehawk, maybe they still do.

Chapter Thirty-Five

Did It Make a Difference, If You Couldn't Tell the Difference?

It was raining. Sometimes it seemed like it had been raining all year, every year, since... Well, you know the one.

The box was on the pavement, slightly off balance because one of the slabs had risen, doubtless because the earth had moved thanks to all the rainwater. The wide kerb was Yorkshire Stone: treacherous, even for someone with a tight-rope walker's balance, in the wet. Being no Blondini, I was sticking to the uneven surface of the pavement. I had called Underworld Limo Hire, and got an answering service. I hadn't realised such things hadn't been replaced completely by automated reply services, with their robotic options. Still, even if you got a conversation nowadays, it was probably with one of AI's finest chat-bots. Did it make a difference if you couldn't tell the difference?

Anyway, I was told I could expect a driver anytime before the next millennium, so I guessed maybe it was an AI voice, after all.

Charon arrived in another antique. A '95 Model Ford Probe, The Ford Capri replacement killed off by being Alan Partridge's[1] car of choice. Besides, although we all know most coupés are the area sales manager's penis substitute, why call it a "probe"? She

---

1. A made-up radio and TV host portrayed by Steve Coogan. No longer popular as Richard Madeley has firmly placed himself beyond parody, by copying Coogan's performances meticulously.

opened the boot and I put the box inside. By this time, it looked as though it had never been opened. I sat in the front, there not being enough room in the back to chastise a drunken sailor – why *was* it "swing a cat", anyway? I'd imagine you'd need quite a lot of room to swing a whip, especially if it was a cat o'nine tails.

My chauffeuse was not in uniform. She'd gone full Ginger Spice in that mini-dress. I wondered how tall she'd be in the platform boots. Charon cocked her head to one side.

'Come on, I'm scary enough, I don't need to be Mel B. Where to, Mr Cowell?'[2]

Maybe I did look a bit like him with my new face and anything but dad-bod, I wouldn't have said so, back in the day.

'I don't actually have an address, but you can take me to Charnel House Head Office.'

---

2. Manager of 1990s all female not-beat combo The Spice Girls, who empowered women and girls by wearing skimpy outfits. whilst singing about their mum and whatever Zig-A-Zig-Ahs were. Cowell also famous for having high-waisted trousers.

'It's in London today. If you wait until tomorrow it will be in Manchester – for the weekend. Monday would be Leeds – maybe even better. Then Wednesday it will be Edinburgh.'

'Why?'

'Well, the Wizard Woman still lives up there. The bill is just about due.'

That wasn't what I had meant, but maybe I didn't really want to know how head office managed to be so mobile.

'The smoke it is, Ginger.'

We didn't speak for quite a while, so I fell asleep.

Chapter Thirty-Six

That's What We Fools Do

By the time I woke up we were passing Hatfield. We had left the North well and truly behind. It wasn't raining this far south. Charon had taken the A1(M). I had expected to cross the Pennines and come down the M1. I asked her just where in London we were going. She said Islington. My heart sank.

'Wharf Road?' I asked, receiving in reply a snort of amused affirmation.

Wharf Road, where Untethered's[1] offices had been before the move from light blue to dark blue on the Monopoly[2] board. Perhaps it was coincidence, but I considered it more likely that Charnel House Publishing, or its Editor-At-Large, was having a joke at my expense.

Charon drove with as little regard for the law as other drivers, playing a near-suicidal game of dodgems on Liverpool Road all the way to the City Road where she upped her game still further and I nearly popped a weasel.[3]

---

1. In book 3, Brontë's Inferno, Moffat, the anti-hero of 'Kyphotic Hall' & 'Mississippi Moffat', murders two footpads on the way back from a brothel, which is located at Untethered's then address... Which is how I know no-one read it.

2. For the benefit of American Readers, British Monopoly is based on geographical locations in London, naturally. The Angel, Islington is light blue and equivalent to Vermont Ave. Mayfair, is dark blue and equivalent to Boardwalk – but much posher.

3. You know how it goes, I bet you're humming it now. What is a weasel doing going pop anyway?

And yet, we survived unscathed, with not too much carnage visible out of the rear windscreen, nor any flashing blue lights in pursuit or attending injured parties. Once we reached Islington, even Charon could not improve the cold-treacle flow of vehicles during the late afternoon pre-rush-hour rush-hour, where the streets of London filled with traffic trying to beat the traffic.

The Probe pulled over at Untethered's former place of business. Naturally, there was nowhere to park. I got out my wallet, figuring I should be paying for this trip. My driver gave me a look that I couldn't decode.

'Don't pay me, Mister Passenger. I'll let you know when – or even if – you need to pay.'

'When will that be?'

'When I get you to the other side.'

Charon drove off to who knew where, the box still in the boot, where I presumed it would be safe enough.

I walked over to the door in the building that had been my publisher's less than a decade ago. As before, there was a very discreet plaque on the crumbling brick. It did not read 'Untethered'. The words etched on the brass, read simply,

> ***The Right Place***

For a second time, I reflected that the building might once have been a chandler's office or a very small manufactory, back in the days when people used words like that. There was no longer a bell beside the door. Instead the door now boasted a brass knocker, in the shape of the vaguely goat's head-like letters of the Charnel House logo.

I lifted the knocker and rather than let it fall I gave it a satisfying "rat-a-tat-tat". However, no-one came to answer it. There was the dynamo hum of an electrical ratchet and the door opened slower than seemed either probable or desirable. No-one stood on the threshold in welcome, or on guard. I rushed in, because that's what we fools do.

Chapter Thirty-Seven

The Broad Arrow

THE PLACE WAS SCARCELY recognisable. The best part of a decade ago there had been stairs and three opaque glazed doors leading off a foyer, whose walls were painted brick. There were a few shelves on one wall, holding copies of the company's published list at that time. 'Kyphotic Hall' was just visible on the highest shelf at the far right-hand end, looking for all the world as though it had been jammed up there minutes before my arrival. I remembered a few dozen copies of my novel ready to sign on a metal desk, with the sort of stacking chair beloved of 1960s schools in front of it. Against one wall, under a dirty – but doubtless listed – Georgian window, stood a tatty three-piece suite, which looked like it might have been stamped underneath with the MOD's broad arrow[1].

Someone less than half my age had rushed in, looking flustered, saying they hadn't expected me so early. I did not say that my early arrival had been prompted by a need to get things over with in order to wait out my hangover in some quiet cafe. Nevertheless, strong coffee was forthcoming. I didn't see anyone else from Untethered, there was a crisis meeting going on behind one of the half-glazed doors. The lettering said 'Board Room'.

---

1. The M.O.D marks every item in its inventory with "The Broad Arrow", right down to the furniture in military accommodation and the cutlery in Married Quarters. Prisoners serving at Their Majesties' pleasure used to wear uniforms marked with a Broad Arrow pattern.

There was the occasional snore to be heard from the other side.

Now, however, everything was all polished concrete floors and sleek furniture devoid of handles, knobs and, indeed, paperwork or books. Even the window was now one of those expensive types where you could see out, but not in. So much for listing. The stairs had been replaced by a lift with a burnished metal door. My reflection looked like something seen in a hall of mirrors. I looked like myself as I had appeared to be only a few short hours ago. I took the strange mirror from my messenger bag and looked at it. Still young and handsome. More handsome than I'd ever been. Did this image exist only in that mirror? Or was my appearance as it always had been? As it was in the lift door, in fact?

The lift opened and there was the Editor-At-Large. Arms outstretched in welcome, ready to give a real Russian bear hug, which he proceeded to inflict on me immediately he stepped into the foyer. Behind him the door closed and the only reflection in it was my own, still – perhaps – distorted.

'Misha, Misha, Misha. So gled you join us! So gled!'

The Scandinavian Bela Lugosi[2] effect was particularly marked. I had preferred his near faultless West Yorkshire twang from the The Fire Station Cafe.

---

2. See footnote, page 7. I know, you didn't read it.

Chapter Thirty-Eight

Just Like That

'Do you think it? We work together? Like Eliot and Pound? Hemingway and Perkins!'[1] The Editor-At-Large of Charnel House really did sound excited. I did my best to calm him down with my own suggestion.

---

1. Maxwell Perkins was the editor of - amongst others -Hemingway, Scott Fitzgerald and William Faulkner. His relationship with Thomas Wolfe was particularly stormy. Perhaps that's why The Editor-In-Chief chooses not to mention it.

'Abbot and Costello?'[2]

'You very funny, Misha. Very funny guy. No more jokes. Is serious business.' He let go of me at last, raised his hand above his head and clicked his fingers.

A large slab of marble popped out of the wall opposite the window and slid to one side. Hella was carrying Begemot over her cleavage. Perhaps she was cold.

'Dah-link! How lovely to see you! She moved the cat's head to address him personally or feline-ly, I couldn't be sure which. 'We're so glad Mickey B has come, aren't we, Beggy-Weggy.'

I swear the cat rolled his eyes. So did I.

'We go in back, Misha. Have things to discussing.'

Hella and Begemot being nearest, they lead the way back through the hole in the marble, which closed behind all four of us with the faintest click. Although I had never set foot in the board room on my last visit to the

---

2. Knockabout, unsophisticated, comedy duo popular in the 1940s. Famous for the baseball routine, 'Who's On First", which may or may not need a question mark.

building. I cannot say I was expecting what was on the other side of the sliding marble.

That is, a scene from the last days of Rome, or perhaps Tinto Brass's[3] infamous bonk-buster, '*Caligula*'. If he'd given it an RSC-style modern (un)dress makeover. Bob Guccione – yes, that one, the Penthouse magazine guy – was the producer of the film.

Grapes were being peeled, some of them were even being eaten. Fruit in general seemed a popular accessory to the various kinds of carnal activity in progress on all sides. Hella gave me a slow wink,

'We never get bored at board meetings, Mickey Boy.'

No-one was entirely nude, even the one-legged man in congress with a person of indeterminate gender by the large fountain in the centre of what might only be called an

---

3. Brass was at least 3rd choice to direct after John Huston. The Italian later said he had been trying to make a Citizen Kane-type film, set in Ancient Rome. He didn't succeed.

atrium, was wearing a single sock, although not on his foot. It really was remarkable the inclusivity on display. The Editor-At-Large smiled with his gin-trap teeth,

'Oh yes, Misha, we are right up to date. All Charnel House employees receive EDI training. Every day for rest of their immortality. We no invent, but wish did.'

I told him his Bela Lugosi impression was terrible and he went bats. Or bat, at least.

Hella laughed, 'What **did** you say to him, Mickey dah-ling? No-one has made him that angry since Universal Pictures cut his walk-on part in "*Hellzapoppin*".[4] The bat flew erratically, now just below the vaulted ceiling, then in a haphazard slalom flight path between the fluted columns holding it up.

I suppose the guests at the orgy were too busy to notice their host's transformation

---

4. Probably the most bonkers Universal Picture ever. And the E-A-L was disappointed? Everyone wants to be in the movies, I suppose

into a frenzied vespertilionine[5] specimen, for no-one looked upwards except the few who were lying on their back. Most likely they had other things on their mind. The Editor-At-Large flapped a few more times, but in an increasingly lethargic manner. He landed, there was a puff of smoke and there he was dressed in a dinner jacket and a fez. I asked him which drugs he was pumping through the air conditioning. He just clapped his hands over his head and the whole orgy disappeared.

Just like that.

---

5. Those who remember the 11 plus know "Cat is to Feline as Cow is to ____?" was a typical question. Luckily for me the second half of the question wasn't "... as Bat is to _____?" I suspected many pupils were given a paper with that version of the question, just to keep them out of grammar school.

Chapter Thirty-Nine

"A-HAR, HAR, HAR."

T HE ROOM REMAINED A Cinecitta[1] style atrium. The grape peelings had vanished from the mosaic floor, which was a faithful reproduction of what certain fragmentary

---

1. Hollywood, Italian-Style. Just outside Rome. Built under the Mussolini regime as he poured money into the movie industry. "Cinema is the most powerful weapon" was the slogan of the day. It applies to the internet nowadays, of course.

fresco finds in Pompeii had promised[2]. Behind the far colonnade, all was in Stygian darkness. For all I knew, every single reveller could have run off into a space the size of an aircraft hangar and still be revelling, only somewhat less noisily.

The Editor-At-Large's fez was at a rather jaunty angle and the dinner suit's trouser stripe looked a little dull. The cuffs showing at the end of the dj's sleeves[3] were quite grubby. Begemot was now standing on his hind legs and Hella was dressed like a magician's assistant. I tried not to look at her legs. They all three looked at me expectantly.

I pointed at my face, 'What the fuck have you done? How long was I in that bloody hospital? What kind of plastic surgery really does make someone look younger?'

---

2. Particularly those found in the Lupanar Brothel. On public display in the Secret Museum in Naples since 2000. Previously by appointment only.

3. No, not Craig Charles, Spoony or any other disc spinner. It's what people used to call a dinner jacket. Formal wear for men – usually. It looked great on women too.

'Think of it ass a golden hello,' Begemot said. 'Ssomething not in the contract.'

'A sweetener for you, Sweetie.' Hella leaned towards me. She must have been cold, but Begemot was now too big to lie on her décolletage. The Editor-At-Large seemed somehow different, more shambling. He said nothing, merely restricting himself to the nervous laugh of a much bigger man.

'You can't operate on people without their permission. No doctor would ever do that.' My voice warbled like a teenage boy's.

The Editor-At-Large finally spoke, 'We have – har, har – plenty of specialists. Everyone comes to us eventually – har, har, har – Mengele, for example, has been with us for a few years. Har. Who says you've had surgery, anyway?'

I took the mirror out of my messenger bag, looked at my impossible image once again. Then I tried to hand it to The Editor-At-Large. He waved it away.

'No reflection on you, but I do not care so much for mirrors, despite appearances. A-har, har, har.'

'Mengele? He wasn't a writer! He was, was...'

'No, har-har, he wasn't.' He swept off the fez and he either threw it somewhere very fast, or it disappeared. He straightened up. The dinner suit seemed a better fit, he started to look more like someone who would have called his outfit a tuxedo. He put an arm around my shoulders,

'Now really, you didn't think I was just in publishing, did you? Even I need a hobby, eternity is awfully boring, even – no, especially – with people like Mengele[4] for company.'

---

4. Herr Doktor Josef Mengele. MD. Nazi, Eugeneicist, awfully nasty fellow. Died of natural causes in Brazil at 67, which just goes to show there is very little justice in this world and may be why so many hope it may be served in the next.

Chapter Forty

Not Even Purgatory

The Editor-At-Large, his arm still draped around my shoulders, said 'Walk with me,' like a high-powered politico in a terrible drama from Netflix.[1] I glanced behind: Hella and Begemot were following. The giant cat was still on his hind legs with a walk that

---

1. You know the kind. The kind that looks and sounds like it was made by a committee of bad writers, or even by AI after digesting everything out of Shondaland since season 2 of Scandal.

reminded me of Groucho's.[2] I was guided into the darkness behind the colonnade.

It wasn't an aircraft hangar. It was a hangar-sized office, one of those places with several hundred pods and two or three glazed wall offices on a gallery looking down on the minions. Of course, there *was* a clearway leading to the glass elevator which in turn gave access to the mezzanine floor where the titans could look down on the rodents in their wheels. Or workstations, if you prefer. Clearly, I was in the company of the titans. Hella and Begemot had caught up and were propelling me through the serried ranks of those working. I half-recognised people I had never met but had seen among the ranks of the infamous. Who knew how good some of portraitists of antiquity had been back in their day? Caligula looked like exactly his bust in the Carlsberg Glyptotech in Copenhagen. That is, like a grumpy nutter.

---

2. Marx, of the Marx Bros (qv) still the only Marxes worth paying attention to.

I stared down at the minions for the few seconds it took the elevator to reach the realm of the Titans. It really was entirely too sophisticated to be called a lift. 360 degree views even as we ascended. No metal frame in sight, no buttons to push.

We spilled out onto the mezzanine in front of the offices, which had no door furniture and were entirely made of glass. The largest had lettering on the outside of the glass. It read 'Woland', Editor At Large', where a door should have been. It opened somehow. The other half of the shop floor was visible from the far side of this, the largest of the inner sancta.

The view was just the same, row upon row of soulless, partitioned "workstations". I could almost see the despair. No-one, nobody, not one person looked up.

I looked at the Editor-In-Chief, 'I'm dead and in Hell, aren't I?'

Begemot guffawed. Hella tittered behind a gloved hand.

'Oh, no, Mickey! This isn't Hell. Why, it's not even Purgatory. And how could you be dead? A contract is a contract, after all.'

'So I'm just mad, then?'

Woland bowed his head. There were two little bumps just above his temples, which he rubbed with his fingertips until they disappeared. When he looked up at me, he winked, 'No, Mickey B, you're not crazy, not yet!'

'This building is crazy, that damn' place up past Malham was crazy.'

Everything was crazy. It was so real. Say that fast and it sounds like "surreal".

'You didn't mention Begemot, Misha. I wonder why?'

Maybe it *was* drugs, a bad trip. Maybe I was still in hospital on a drip. Or someone had mickey-d my drink and the ketamine was never going to wear off.

'What's so crazy about a cat walking on its hind legs?'

Hella's glove stroked my cheek, 'That's the spirit, Dah-link!'

Chapter Forty-One

"What kind of beast do you think I am?"

All the furniture in all three offices was white, even the partner's desk. There was no privacy whatever, even for the the three Titans. Aside from the glossy white office furnishings, there were two large sofas with a coffee table just within reach of anyone sitting on them, if they perched on the edge of the seat and had disproportionately long arms.

'Coffee, Misha?' Woland cocked his head to one side as if listening for the faint sound of something or other.

Hella winked at me, 'Something stronger for our newest recruit, I think.'

Begemot lifted his tail to his mouth and chewed at it, before succumbing to a coughing fit and bringing up a furball the size of tumbleweed. 'Me too,' he said. The lift doors opened on the mezzanine outside the office. An old-fashioned brass and glass drinks trolley came in followed by two faces familiar to me. We had signed on with Untethered at the same time. We had only met in person once, around Limehouse.

We shot a promotional video starring a latter-day version of The Three Stooges[1]; Jim O'Connell, Larry Avarice and me. I had wandered round a churchyard spouting nonsense about Kyphotic Hall, Jim had used the same location. Larry walked up and down the Thames river bank. He'd have been bet-

---

1. Another unsophisticated comedy act. Not even as funny as Abbot & Costello.

ter off mudlarking[2] for all the money our books made. The enterprising film-maker also recorded the three of us in his tiny office, 'talking shite' – as Jim so memorably put it in his Clydebank patois. The video of that conversation never did appear. I wouldn't have been surprised if it had turned up on some web-site as an example of what not to say when the camera is running. Maybe it will one day.

JIm gave a nod and said, 'Whit'll it be?' Larry had a tea-towel over his arm and a sommelier's long apron, he gave a bow, then raised an eyebrow.

I asked for a single malt. Woland said 'Make that two.'

'Ye's are wantin' a double, right?' Jim's jaw jutted as he looked Woland in the eye.

'No, Jim, is it? I want a single malt too.'

'So yis're wantin' two double single malts?'

---

2. Popular in the Victorian era, plodging through the mud beside the Thames looking for valuables and scrap washed up by the river.

'Two single single malts!' The Editor-At-Large's spittle almost landed on Larry's pristine white tea-towel, but he stepped aside gracefully.

'Ach, why did ye no' say so, in the furrst place.'

Whilst Jim prepared the drinks, he grumbled to himself. It sounded like 'Getifah ya bassah'. Perhaps it was Gaelic. Jim put the drinks onto a silver salver that Larry had liberated from somewhere on the trolley.

'And the leddy'll be wontin' a snifter hersel', no?' Jim smiled at Hella. At least I thought it was a smile. She smiled back anyway, and asked for a Mississippi Mud Slide.

Begemot hissed, 'Saucer of Bailey's.'

'How's aboot a please?' Jim said, 'Manners maketh... achh, ferget it!'

Somehow Jim managed to produce the two flavours of ice-cream necessary and, of course, the bourbon wasn't a problem. Jim and Larry went through the silver salver routine for Hella's cocktail. Jim was just bending down to put Begemot's saucer of Bailey's on the white marble floor, when Begemot hissed again, 'What kind of beast do you think I am?'

Begemot held the saucer in both paws and tipped what must have been a third of a bottle of the cream liqueur down his throat. I hoped he wasn't an angry drunk.

Chapter Forty-Two

The Lucky Ones

Woland downed his malt. I sipped mine. Jim and Larry went through the salver routine and replenished the Editor-At-Large's drink.

'Well this is nice. Old friends meeting again.' Woland sipped at his malt this time.

'Is it? What do you think, Jim? Larry? What in hell are you doing here anyway?' I wasn't used to whiskey. Especially not the stuff that cost more per drop than AB negative in a Transylvanian Blood Bank.

Jim said something incomprehensible again, 'Gett tae Fuh', this time.

Larry gave a curt bow, clicked his heels and said 'In Hell. Exactly.'

Woland looked me in the eye and shook his head, 'I have a special place for all you ex-Untethered authors.'

'In your heart, no doubt.' I said.

He looked at me in horror. Hella tittered behind a gloved hand. It must have been enough to make a cat laugh, because Begemot did. Woland recovered his equanimity. I had often wondered what that actually looked like. In the Editor-at-Large's case, it meant a straightening of the spine, a roll of the shoulders and the smile of a paedophile at the school gate on his lips. I shuddered. He clasped an arm around my shoulders,

'Oh no, it's more "everywhere and nowhere, baby."'

He'd ear-wormed me again, just like he had

with Vincent Price's laugh. I wondered once more what I'd got myself into. Whatever it was, I doubted there would be any kind of silver lining at all.

I resolved to ask a bit more about what – exactly – I was supposed to do. Woland's smile became still more unnerving.
'So you didn't read all of the contract?'
I spelled it out for him, ' T-L-D-N-R'.
Everyone but Jim and Larry burst out laughing.
'Oh, capital! Just capital! We knew he was the one, didn't we Hella?'
'Oh yes, Dah-link. Yes – we – did.'

'Tell him, Begemot. Tell him what he'll be doing.'
The huge cat licked the back of his paw and wiped it across what would have been its forehead if it weren't – well – a cat's head. 'You're going to be writing ALL the booksss.'
'I know that already, you told me that yourself, Woland.'

The Editor-At-Large clapped his hands next to his ear, like some demented Bulgarian copying a Flamenco dancer in a Seville tourist trap bar. Jim pushed the trolley forward, reached into the second shelf, pulled out an open lap-top and placed it on the silver salver that Larry had yet again produced from under his waistcoat, or somewhere equally unlikely. Larry glided across the shining marble floor and presented the laptop towards me.

'Press any button you like.' Woland said.

Even though I pressed the 'esc' key, there was no escape, and I was still in the office, standing in front of a laptop. A massive banner headline came up on the screen like the ones the hackers in the '80s used to splash up on a hooky Amiga game, even though most of those same hackers ended up being caught because of them.

> "Congratulations Player Infinity, You have written the next million books – Thanks to AI. Brought to you by Data Kobold"

I gasped, walked over to look down at the toiling minions. "So what are *they* all doing?"

It was Larry who spoke.

'The lucky ones are keeping Charnel House going. Paying bills, playing the stock markets, starting wars, pandemics and "new" energy initiatives.'

'Aye, right.' Jim said.

'And those who aren't numbered among the – no-doubt very few – lucky?'

Woland's smile widened and let a fang peep out at either end. 'Why! The same as they always did, when they trod a more temporal plane.'

'And what's that?' Although I suspected I knew the answer.

'Come now, Mishka. They are writing all the books that will **never** be published.'

Chapter Forty-Three

"Or you wouldn't be reading this"

'What on earth for?' It seemed pointless.

Hella drawled, 'Perhaps you might want to rephrase that, Dah-link.'

'Why then?'

But it was Begemot who gave the answer. 'We are running out of good booksssss.'

I asked what he meant. He looked at Woland, who spread his arms wide as he spoke.

'There are very few books that – well, say anything new. We got too big, here at Charnel House.'

There wasn't time to be going into the concept of 'here', given the impossibility of our location. I must have looked puzzled.

'There are other publishers. Of course there are, there are independents, very few of which sell any books. We do keep a look out for them.' He nodded towards the drones working below. We have one or two people transcribing those.

'What? Like Project Gutenburg?'

'In a way, yes. AI needs everything. Or its output will all be the same, until or unless AI learns how to be truly creative. I'm beginning to think it may never happen.'

I laughed. I could taste the bitterness in my mouth. 'Isn't it all the same now?'

'Well, yes, Misha. Yes, it is. That's why the others are writing all the books that will never be published. We don't even edit them, AI digests it all.'

'In the hope of giving Artificial Intelligence some creativity? Isn't that dangerous?'

Woland sighed, 'Misha, Misha, Misha... Isn't that my job? Evil mastermind?'

I looked at him. Wondered if and when I would ever wake up. 'What am I *really* doing here?'

He pointed at Hella and Begemot, 'Can't you guess?'

I couldn't. So I didn't. I just shrugged like an adolescent caught lying.

'I want some company, conversation, someone to have an argument with.' The big cat hissed and so did Hella. 'Calm down. It's not replacement it's... what do they call it? Refreshing the top-down hierarchy. No... No... Employing a consultant, that's it!'

His eyes glittered and I knew he meant it.

'Come on! I want to show you something. Thank you, Jim, thank you, Larry.'

We headed toward the lift. Woland held up a hand when Begemot – but not Hella – tried to follow. Her look would have killed us both, if the Editor-At-Large weren't – as I suspected – immortal, and I a construct of my own imagination.

We stepped into the lift. Woland said 'Going up. Right to the very top.'

The ride lasted much longer than I expected. We stepped out. We were no longer in Kansas, Kensington and definitely not Islington. It was a high tower. So high that the air was thin. I could see all of London and the commuter belt beyond. The horizon was so far away, I wasn't sure it was even there.

'You're going to offer me the whole world, aren't you?'

'No, Misha. No. I've tried that one before, it didn't work then.'

'What then?' I said.

'I'm going to give you a coin.'

He held out a scruffy, battered metal disc. 'Take it.' he said.

I took it; turned it over, there were faint markings, nothing I could decipher.

'Come to the edge.' He took my arm as though we were professorial colleagues intent on a deep philosophical discussion on the way to lunch. I didn't resist.

There was no railing or barrier, nothing to hold on to, just the edge of a building that disappeared to nothing at the point were it reached the ground.

'You can jump now. If you want. You know who would be driving the ambulance. You could pay her.'

I leaned forward a little. He held onto me just enough to stop me toppling, but not enough to stop me jumping off. I stayed teetering.

'Or you could jump later... Blow your head off. Take enough drugs to see off Jim, Jimi or Janis.[1] Step in front of a train. As long as you've got that obol, d'you see?'

I did see. I took the coin – and I still have it. Obviously. Or you wouldn't be reading this, would you?

---

[1] The three Js: Morrison, Hendrix and Joplin. All 27 years old and dead from overindulgence of some kind. In some respects a great career move, as they made more records and money after they died. I'd rather have had the music they never got the chance to make, myself.

Epilogue

What happened to the box? As I haven't spent my obol yet, if Charon still has the box, perhaps she'll let me open it on the last journey. Maybe the story of the box is in the box. Or not in the box. I may never know. I haven't asked the Editor-At-Large yet. He just wants to talk about philosophy, quantum physics and ph-ootball...

Socrates is his favourite player[1]. He says Pele "only" played football. It's going to be a long eternity.

---

1. Brilliant Brazilian footballer, qualified M.D and political activist. Died of alcohol-related causes at 57. "Go hard, just in case you have to go early" must have been his philosophy.